GENUINE REASON FOR SALE

GENUINE REASON FOR SALE

A NOVEL BY

Jennifer Melrose

JOHN MURRAY

First published 1985
by John Murray (Publishers) Ltd
50 Albemarle Street, London W1X 4BD

Typeset by Inforum Ltd, Portsmouth
Printed and bound in Great Britain
by the Bath Press, Bath

British Library CIP Data
Melrose, Jennifer
Genuine reason for sale : a novel.
I. Title
823'.914[F] PR6063.E43/
ISBN 0–7195–4212–X

Contents

Illustrations by Christine Bousfield

Author's Note

Since the great revival of interest in the horse over the last two decades or so, books about its schooling, welfare, upkeep and history have been legion. Biographies of those stars – both human and equine – who have 'made it to the top' in show-jumping, dressage, eventing, racing and sundry other activities, regularly dazzle us with their achievement of the ultimate.

This is a book for all those countless ordinary people who have simply owned and loved a horse or pony – or wanted to.

I make no apologies for the so-called sentimentality of approach, for I have found in my own horses a co-operation and nobility of spirit that is all too often lacking elsewhere.

The setting and the characters in this book are entirely imaginary and bear no relation to any real person or actual situation.

My grateful thanks are due to Mrs Rosa Brennan for her accurate and painstaking typing, to my many equestrian friends for their unfailing patience, and to my husband, without whose quiet encouragement and daily practical help this book could never have been written.

To the Memory of
TESS

1 · The Gate

'You all right?' a faint voice reached me from a million light years away.

Drifting weightlessly in space, I looked down at myself as I answered.

'Y–yes, I think so.'

The sour-sweet smell of horse sweat brought me back to earth. I was sitting on it.

Or rather, half lying, my left toe neatly hooked, ballet-like, in the offside stirrup. The *off*side stirrup?

There is a line somewhere in the Koran which says 'The expression in a horse's eyes is like a blessing . . .' This one, standing blessedly still, was gazing round and down at me with a look of startled concern while breathing gently into my face in true Woodhouse fashion.

Gradually my eyes focused. Above me, the branches of a hawthorn, pale ecru with Autumn's near-death, embroidered a lacy leaf-motif on the blue damask of the sky. My hard hat, true to its Approved Safety Standards, was quietly protecting the blonde heads of a clump of dandelions some six feet away.

'Everybody comes off sooner or later,' an instructress had once said crisply in her best British Horse Society manner. 'It's better to get straight back up and no nonsense.'

I eased my left foot from its curious position in the drooping offside stirrup, for once blessing the chesnut's preference for immobility – so often a source of exasperation in the past – and braced myself to rise on my right leg.

It wasn't there.

There was nothing at all unusual about that bright August morning to suggest that my life was about to be changed irrevocably. Unless it was Webster's strange reluctance to be caught. Webster's illustrious sire was repeatedly named in the *Horse and Hound* as the infallible begetter of progeny that would 'go to the top in any sphere'. Webster, however, as far back as a yearling, had firmly settled for the fair to middling. It was usually easier to amble amiably across the paddock when called than to use up energy in pointless evasion.

I had spent most of the morning grimly turning out the cellar. For months a stale, mushroom-like odour had wafted up the stairs and through the cracks of the closed door.

My worst fears were realised. Sleazy damp rot oozed from the old timbers and multi-coloured fungi festooned the deeper recesses of the walls with a profusion of pattern and formations that would have held me transfixed with their macabre beauty, had I been able to hold down the nausea long enough. Rolls of mushy wallpaper and cardboard boxes, umpteen old wine bottles (empty), rusty tins of congealed paint (full), three ancient lawnmowers and a cracked Victorian lavatory bowl, bedecked with roses and forget-me-nots ('patent applied for 1888') made their way into plastic wrappings, the boot of the car and the local rubbish tip.

The walls, stripped of their fungoid impressionism with a sharp knife and a shaking hand, revealed a situation I thought best not to mention to George until after a good meal – *long* after a good meal. By mid-day the entire house, the car and I reeked of rotten mushrooms and decay.

Fresh air, that was what I needed. A quick sluice with Wright's Coal Tar soap later, I was staggering accompanied by a miscellany of spiders (most of whom had thought it prudent to bring their cobwebs with them on this unexpected emigration) in search of Rosemary.

Rosemary, to state the obvious, was in the stable yard where she coped cheerfully with a dozen or so horses and three working pupils – a euphemism for a certain type of teenager who 'wants to work with horses' and loves riding them but often little else connected with the hard grind of their welfare.

'It's such a lovely day,' I said. 'I fancy a hack – perhaps a turn round the fields and back. Like to join me?' 'The fields' usually meant the hundred or so acres of our own land, and often provided Rosemary with a welcome break from her routine without interrupting it unduly. It also gave the working pupils the chance to practise that alien and terrifying experience known as using your own initiative.

'Love to,' said Rosemary, putting down the wheelbarrow and easing her shoulders. 'Which horse do you want to ride?'

It was a question which never ceased to catch me by surprise, and send an odd quiver down my back. All my life, I had yearned for a horse of my own. Now I had twelve to choose from. For, after years as a teacher, I had at last followed my heart and started a small riding school giving specialised tuition.

'Something easy-going and uncomplicated,' I said. 'Cleaning out that cellar has knocked the stuffing out of me.'

'Mm-m,' said Rosemary. 'I think I can smell it.'

And so it was I went in search of Webster, the easy-going, and encountered my first oddity of the day. Webster, who usually obliged by dropping his nose into the headcollar, the action requiring the minimum energy, took a full twenty minutes to catch, and twice actually cantered away. Clearly he did not think my idea of a turn round the fields a good one. Was it the fungoid aroma still clinging to my hair and hands? Or . . . well, even the most hardened of horsey types have been known to admit that horses sometimes seem to have a sixth sense.

It is an experience known to most of us that the anticipation of an unpleasant task is often more exhausting than the execution of it. In fact, when one gets down to it, it's not so bad after all, and can even be quite enjoyable. Webster was one of those individuals who discovered this truism almost daily. Once he got all four legs responding in the appropriate sequence, tail arched and neck nicely flexed, the bit nestling more or less where it should be, he usually decided that a turn round the fields was quite a pleasant diversion, especially if the weather was fine.

That glorious Autumn day was no exception. The sun shone benignly with scarcely a hint of the season of mists and mellow fruitfulness to come, and marred only by a gusty, playful breeze which sent the drying leaves skittering across our path.

Rosemary, mounted on The Squire, our splendid dapple grey, set the pace. It was exactly what I needed: a brisk trot, a leisurely canter, the blustering wind clearing the cellar-stench from my lungs and the cobwebs from my mind.

Our fields were showing a scarlet petticoat of poppies where the hay-makers had skirted the edges. I wondered how many of Burns' wee sleekit, cowerin', tim'rous beasties had found refuge there, and whether the sparrow-hawk hovering almost motionless above us had spotted them. Already the hawthorn hedges were aglow with hips and haws; a flurry of little birds flew up from their meal of thistle seeds, too fast to be identified.

'The cellar walls aren't *that* bad,' I thought, at peace with the world. 'We'll get a local man in to give us a quotation. We could even grow mushrooms down there!' I giggled at the thought of the bumper crop.

By now, Rosemary and The Squire were well ahead. Webster with that crafty intuition recognised by all riders, had sensed my pre-occupation and settled down to a languid jog-trot. Suddenly he shot forwards. As we turned along the side of the last field, the playful breeze, gathering force past a narrow wood, had, like many a comedian, gone too far, and with a mighty guffaw, buffeted him up the tail.

'Watch the gate,' called out Rosemary. 'It's swinging a bit – the wind's rising.'

Gates, as any farmer will tell you, belong to a species of their own. Masquerading as mere movable fences, they can be obstinate, drunken, menacing, crafty, chained up, broken down, slyly coming up behind you, insolently slamming in your face. This one had clearly had ambitions as a youngster to be a metronome. Encouraged by the woodwind section it swung back and forth from field to lane with a rhythmic precision that would have won acclaim in the Albert Hall.

Rosemary and The Squire timed it to perfection, slipping nimbly through to my silent applause. Not to be outdone, Webster, offended tail aloft, put on a most uncharacteristic spurt and got through on the off-beat, only to get a smart thwack on the rump as he reached the tarmac. The gate was excelling itself, swinging much too far out into the lane.

'I'd better fasten that up properly,' I muttered. 'It could cause a serious accident.'

Still startled but obedient, Webster waited while I reached for the catch. He quite liked shutting gates; it often provided a few precious moments of genuine immobility. Neither of us was prepared for this one's devilish next move. A sudden gale-force blast whipped the heavy iron back into the field dragging me sideways from the saddle until I hung suspended between animal and gate. Then, like a slow-motion film, saddle and girth began to slip. Webster, staggering awkwardly off-balance, his head and neck grotesquely twisted by my frantic grip on the reins, gave a violent shrug to rid himself of this final insult to his dignity, and my right hip hit the ground.

It took quite a long time to dawn on Rosemary and me that I genuinely could not 'get back up and no nonsense'. Old habits die hard. We laughed a little shakily while we waited for the feeling to come back into my right leg. It did not. My eyes told me it was still there, my trembling fingers explored its outline, but any signals from my brain to the offending limb drew a complete blank. I could neither kneel on it, stand on it nor even move it – and there was no pain.

It is amazing how we British are always at our best pretending that all's well when it is not. While Rosemary took the two horses back and went to fetch transport, I sat on the grass verge and watched the cars go by. Their occupants either waved, nodded or ignored according to their real or imagined status. I waved, nodded or ignored as courtesy required. A van driver, cruising by on a go-slow job yelled, 'Lost yer 'orse, 'ave yer?'

'Yes,' I chirped back. 'Got a spare one in the back?'

No-one seemed to think it the least bit strange that a lone horse-rider should be sitting on the grass in the oriental Royal Posture – one leg elegantly stretched, the other doubled under – and no-one thought to ask if I needed help.

The wait in Emergency Reception seemed interminable. Stripped of my jodhpurs and boots I lay flat out on a narrow, raised bed; Rosemary in jeans and green wellies sat nearby. A nurse bustled in, in an aura of Dettol and starch, gave us a long, hard look, opened a window and rustled back out.

'I'm so sorry,' Rosemary said faintly, 'I should have changed into my proper riding gear, but you seemed so anxious to get away.'

I had interrupted Rosemary, I now recalled, in the middle of mucking out. There was no doubt about it; the pristine, white-painted room was steadily acquiring the aroma of a stable.

I turned awkwardly towards her. It was the first time I had looked at her properly since my fall. She was pale with shock and anxiety. Efficient horsewoman she might be, but she was very young.

'Don't worry,' I said, 'They're used to funny smells in a place like this. I must still be pretty niffy myself after that cellar. They'll probably . . .'

At that moment the pain struck.

A shaft of agony tore through my hip and seared its way down my leg to jerk my knee and foot violently upwards. A throbbing echo of the spasm made its way up my side to my armpit and a spurt of vomit finished the sentence.

Rosemary fled for help. I was left alone to toss and turn and cry out for all eternity.

'Keep quite still,' a firm voice said, and an antiseptic-looking young man administered a sharp, almost imperceptible jab to my rear. Slowly, a woozy, gentle calmness settled over me. He leaned across to place light fingers on my wrist.

'Horse muck and mushrooms,' I murmured helpfully.

'Er – quite,' he said, and opened another window a bit.

The doctor who brought the X-rays had been ominously cheerful.

'You gave yourself quite a nasty bang,' he said, 'Knocked the top off your femur – cracked a few odds and ends as well. I'm afraid you'll have to stay with us. We'll operate tomorrow.'

I hadn't really taken in the details.

'Will I be able to ride again?' I asked.

'Good heavens, yes. We'll probably do a sort of hip-replacement job. Some people have it done specially so that they can get back to the Hunt.'

But the hours that followed were a nightmare of vivid pain and shadowy, spectre-like shapes, one of them George's lined and anxious face drifting in and out of my consciousness.

Unbelievably, the morning came and with it a group of crisp, efficient figures. Gentle hands lifted me on a trolley, an upside-down face said, 'Won't be long now,' and suddenly I was under a canopy of brilliant light.

Never in my whole life had I even considered oblivion, but I yearned for it now. The brown eyes and black brows between the cotton mask and cap were unmistakably Asian and infinitely wise. Unasked, I raised my arm for the needle and . . .

'How are you feeling now?' asked a pretty, blonde nurse. 'Would you like a drink?'

Behind her the ward was alive with the laughter and chatter

of Visiting Time. I was back, the pain had gone and I slept.

'Right, Mrs Melrose. Up you get! We're going to take a turn round the ward.'

I stared stupidly at the white-coated figure. Grey haired but straight backed she smiled down at me, a pair of aluminium crutches in her hand.

'I'm from physiotherapy. We're going to get you up today.'

'She's mad,' I thought, but succumbed to being manipulated out of bed and into an upright position, while she explained, as if to a five-year-old, the mechanics of gripping, balancing and moving. Sweating profusely, I took a shaky step and then another. It worked! There was a round of applause from the nearby beds.

Encouraged by this unexpected phenomenon, I considered a wobbly pilgrimage down the centre of the ward. At the other end, a fragile figure was coming towards me, similarly equipped. Strain and pain had etched deep lines into the thin face and her lips were clenched white with the effort.

'Poor soul,' I thought. '*She*'s been through it. If she can do it, so can I.'

I balanced myself very carefully and lifted my left crutch in greeting with a smile. She raised her right one and smiled wanly back. It was several seconds before I realised she was a mirror.

Back in my bed, I was visited by the consultant and his semi-circle of silent, respectful acolytes.

'I hear you've been up and about,' he said.

I glowed with exhausted pride.

'I will be able to ride again then?' I asked. He seemed to take a long time to screw the top on his pen and place it precisely in the exact position in his breast pocket.

'Now turn slowly on your side,' he said quietly, avoiding my eyes. Painfully I did so, towards the wall and window.

Outside a stray branch from a shrub was etched against a leaden sky as the first ominous rumblings of thunder came, and rain, like great tear-drops, blurred its leaf-motif image against the window pane.

2 · Bracken

It is a truth universally acknowledged, as Jane Austen would have said, that a man's best friend is not his dog but a benevolent bank manager. There came a time when, with their customary old world courtesy, Messrs Coutts and Co. of the Strand, expressed their continuing concern about my welfare, but wondered respectfully whether George might care to call and discuss with them the various reasons why our cash flow no longer did.

My slow progress from in-patient to out-patient to ex-patient steadily revealed a simple fact: my accident had cut off not only the head of my femur but also the source of my income as well.

After two vain attempts to find a suitable deputy at short notice to run the riding school – the first was addicted to nipping out for quick one, and the second, a divorcee, was apt to burst into tears over Sir Philip Sidney's sonnets – I had made a snap decision to close it down. Pupils were directed to other establishments but the horses they had ridden presented a more complicated problem. Riderless, they continued to eat their way through mountains of bran, maize, barley, oats, sugar-beet, hay and my bank balance. Winter, as every reader of *Horse and Hound* will tell you, is not the best season for selling horses.

George returned from his interview at Messrs Coutts and Co. in possession of two clear facts out of the welter of figures: our bank statement had changed colour, and Mr Thompson, the manager, more than usually interested in our equine liabilities, had a small daughter who 'wanted to jump'.

'Bracken,' I said triumphantly.

'What?' said George irritably, for he too had changed colour over the last few hours.

'We've got to get rid of some of them,' I said, warming to my theme. 'So why not sell him Bracken? At least then he'll know we're *trying*,' I added darkly.

Bracken was one of our show pieces, not because of any particular physical beauty. He was simply a Welsh pony of somewhat indeterminant bay-brown. His two great assets were a complete contempt for all things on wheels, be they motor-bike, car, tractor or sundry H.G.V., and a happy willingness to jump anything in sight without stopping or 'running out'. He was game for anything from four inches to four feet, and as they say, bombproof in traffic.

George brightened visibly.

'We'll have him down to lunch – if he'll come,' he said. 'Then he can suss the situation and see the pony as well.'

I wasn't so sure about that one. Coutts' renowned old world courtesy had been acquired as everyone knew from years of association with a Renowned and illustrious clientele. Who knew what regal repasts they had enjoyed in the pursuit of duty? One thing was certain, the chef would not be leaning shakily on a stick with one hand, while tossing the Crêpes Suzettes with the other.

'Oh, come on,' said George, 'It's worth a try. Mrs B will help.'

Mrs B as it turned out, was not only an expert at 'doing' our establishment, but a dab hand at chicken croquettes as well. A tentative menu was devised –

Soup	(tinned, but disguised with a dash of herbs and a dollop of sherry).
Chicken croquettes	(prepared by Mrs B and lurking craftily at the ready under the grill).
Petits pois	(frozen, but tossed in the best Scottish unsalted butter).
Potatoes	(par-boiled and placed in the oven ready to crisp. N.B. switch on oven as car enters drive).
Pineapple Cheesecake	(smuggled in surreptitiously from the Swiss Centre, Leicester Square).
Real Coffee	(poured from Gran's real silver coffee pot, with the dent to the offside of the guest).

The whole to be served on the *pièce de résistance*, Mrs B's hand crocheted lace tablecloth (three star motif in white).

The drinks I left to George.

'A Dry Sack and Blue Nun would probably do,' he said.

Mr Thompson, as it happened, could spare us a couple of hours the following Tuesday, provided that we could pick him up at the local station and get him back in time for a Board meeting that afternoon.

We could, and Operation Bracken was on.

A surprised Welsh pony, unaware that he was about to become the Star Attraction found himself coaxed back from several happy months of pottering in the paddock to the near-forgotten routine of coat grooming, tail brushing, mane smoothing, hoof trimming and even nose wiping. He succumbed to it all with his usual aplomb and obligingly went round and round the lunge rein with appropriate concentration. These two-legged humans he had long since discovered were a weird lot.

Mrs B meanwhile started a systematic grooming of the house – well, the parts of it the manager would actually see.

Hoovering, cleaning and polishing, she banished the cat from the immaculate floor, and found loo paper to match the walls.

I for my part, put my mind to the serious business of What to Wear. Nothing *new* under the circumstances (I made a face at myself in the mirror – I hadn't got anything new). Nothing over fancy: I mustn't look like the sort of female who would make her frivolous way through a colourful overdraft. And shoes? I wondered if for once I could risk two-inch heels. My hospital-specified stick was exactly thirty-three inches long (including rubber safety grip). But then, I mused, maybe the odd genuine totter might further our cause a bit.

Rummaging through the drawers in search of my best tights I found a bundle of photographs. That was it. All our horses had been recorded in Kodacolour at some time or other. I fished them out from their various hiding places and numbered my selection. One: Bracken, calm and reliable, trotting down a lane with a ten-year-old on his back. Two: Bracken, alert and reliable, clearing a coloured pole with a twelve-year old on his back. Three: Bracken, relaxed and reliable, negotiating a traffic jam with myself on his back ('Such a *useful* size, 14 hands') and Four: Bracken, patient and reliable, being dug out of a three-foot snow drift with no-one on his back.

I popped them in an envelope and hid them in the bureau drawer, where I could happen to find them when the occasion arose.

The day dawned cold and grey but mercifully dry, having been preceded by forty-eight hours of non-stop rain which had turned the paddocks, the drive and the lane into a muddy mess.

Bracken, his neat little hooves given a final sheen with Cherry Blossom boot polish, was popped into the barn to be let out into the small front paddock by Rosemary at precisely 12.30, as she left for her half-day off. The small, front paddock, we had already discovered, made an excellent show-case. With its back-drop of trees and the old house, whichever animal it contained invariably drew cries of 'Oh-oh!' and 'Ah-h-h' and 'Isn't he sweet!'

Mr Thompson emerged on to our local station platform at 12.15 precisely seeming strangely incongruous in his pinstripes and city-cut overcoat. Even the pigskin briefcase had an alien, almost ominous look.

'Ah, that country air,' he said inhaling deeply. 'Quite intoxicating,' and he smiled with just the right balance of business-like benevolence as befitted a visit to the domicile of one of their Lesser Accounts.

On the short journey he noted the properties for sale, those under offer and the small number sold. Prices and rates, George observed faintly, were much higher now the line had been electrified.

We finally turned into our drive and towards our rambling old house. The cloak of bright Virginia creeper it usually wore had long become threadbare, but a glory of winter jasmine cuddled it lovingly round the door.

'Ah-h-h,' said Mr Thompson, 'A delightful property.'

'Yes, we're very fond of it,' said George. 'And, by the way, there's the pony I told you about in the small paddock over there.'

We gazed obediently over the fence; there was nothing but damp, untrodden grass and an overflowing water butt.

'These native breeds are absolute experts at camouflage,' I said brightly. 'He's probably watching us from behind somewhere. Do come in and take off your things – there's plenty of time.'

George rushed round the car to open the door chauffeur-wise. 'She's forgotten to let him out,' I hissed. 'Better do it now.'

Inside the house, the invisible Mrs B had done us proud. A splendid log fire crackled in the grate and coaxed an answering gleam from the lavender-waxed floor. Our modest *objets d'art* were strategically placed where they could be viewed in comfort from the settee.

Divested of his coat, Mr Thompson eased his pinstripes and stretched appreciative hands to the blaze.

'You don't often see a real log fire like this these days,' he said.

'No,' I agreed, 'but then we – er – grow our own.'

There was a silence and no sign of George.

'Terrible weather we've had lately,' I volunteered.

'Yes, but I suppose we can't expect much else at this time of the year.'

'Still, at least it's stayed dry for your visit.'

'Yes.'

Another silence.

Desperately I craned towards the window.

'If you watch from here, you'll probably see Bracken go by – such a sweet, reliable pony.'

'Oh good.'

There was a crash as the door swung open with a blast of cold air. George stood with a twig tangled in his hair.

'My God, he really *has* gone!' he gasped with a fine disregard for the basic rules of English usage when addressing bank managers. 'The gate's still padlocked, so he hasn't been stolen, but I can't find a gap in the fencing anywhere.'

It took only a split second for the enormity of the situation to sink in. A loose pony on the public highway was a serious matter indeed, incurring, as it did, a heavy fine. And if it should be involved in an accident . . . my heart missed a beat. Bracken was not insured; his months of happy idleness in the paddock had not warranted it. Visions of dented cars, prostrate cyclists and inert, bleeding ponies flashed before my eyes. Then there was the possibility of vets' bills, astronomical at the best of times – I knew the colour was draining from my face.

Mr Thompson was watching me closely. Was his trained mind totting it up already?

'The car!' I cried in shrill un-hostess-like tones. 'You must get him off the roads. He can't have gone far in that short time.'

'It'll take two of us,' said George distractedly, 'one to drive back, the other to lead him.'

Mr Thompson promptly showed what sterling stuff bank managers are made of.

'Get going then, both of you,' he said. 'Don't mind me; I'm

more than comfortable here.' He reached for the Daily Telegraph and George, on an impulse, thrust a bottle and glass into his hands, and dropped a packet of cashew nuts into his lap.

'Thanks, Mr Thompson,' he said, 'with a bit of luck we won't be too long.'

As I grabbed the headcollar and lead rein already strategically placed behind the kitchen door, the homely smell of lightly browning potatoes wafted from the oven.

I sensed from the start it would be a hopeless task. Our own lane stretched away in a grey-green ribbon and every road we turned into revealed the same blank emptiness. To make matters worse, a steady drizzle had settled in, and most of the local population seemed to have disappeared with the pony.

A lone Mohican, with green hair-dye streaking his face as he investigated the belching broken exhaust of his moped 'adn't seen nuffink since 'e copped this bleedin' lot, and an elderly gentleman exercising a reluctant spaniel regretted he could not converse with us as he had mislaid his hearing aid, cumbersome things.

We drove fairly fast, George's eyes grimly on the road, mine scanning every corner, hedge, gateway, drive, nook or cranny where a native breed could demonstrate his indigenous ability for camouflage.

'It's no use,' I said flatly. 'We may as well go back. I think he's probably gone round the side of the house, through the spinney and back to his pals in the field.'

Apart from the anxiety of the missing Bracken another little worry was niggling at the back of my mind. By now, Mrs B would have slipped discreetly out of the back door, anxious not to be seen as a possible expendable asset. What would a bank manager really be doing left alone in somebody else's house? Suppose he went in search of the loo and walked in on the unmade beds instead – neglected as they were in the morning's feverish preparations? Where *had* I left that pile of dirty shirts? And the bureau – crammed with personal correspondence –

would he notice the pile of bills in the left pigeon-hole most of them printed conspicuously in red?

Mr Thompson as it turned out when we returned, was deeply engrossed in his own affairs, his open briefcase at his knees. Beside him the bottle was still full and the glass still empty.

'You gave me the wrong bottle,' he said drily, 'and I hadn't got a corkscrew. Did you find your pony?'

I could only shake my head.

'No,' said George glumly, 'Not a sign of him. We think he might have gone through the woods and out into the fields, but it's anybody's guess.'

'Is this animal valuable?' asked Mr Thompson re-arranging the papers on his knee.

George winced. It was a delicate matter he had hoped to raise cautiously under more auspicious circumstances.

'Er – about seven hundred or so,' he said.

Mr Thompson's hand hesitated mid-thrust into his briefcase, then he pressed the catch with a decisive and authoritative click. Clearly, he was on his home ground – assets and liabilities, profit and loss, with special emphasis on the last.

'Then we'd better get organised,' he said. 'Have you any spare boots and something waterproof? If the three of us fan out, we're sure to find something.'

I was transfixed with astonishment. A nagging pain was beginning to make its way down my right leg from my hip, but this, I felt, was not the time to mention it.

We must have looked an incongruous trio as we made our slippery way through the winding paths of the spinney. George, in combat suit and cap (army surplus) went warily ahead in true jungle warfare fashion. The shifting shadows of branches with the play of light on his back almost convinced me he carried a gun.

Mr Thompson, enveloped in George's dark grey duffel coat, his head and face hidden in the cowl-like hood, looked strangely ecclesiastical as he passed under the vaulted arches of the trees, the whole effect somewhat marred by his ponderous progress in George's enormous gumboots.

I brought up the rear wearing long-discarded riding gear under the canopy of a bright yellow cycling cape. As I did not possess any waterproof headwear, a plastic bag with its edges rolled up over my ears, proclaimed that we did our shopping at Safeways.

By common consent it was decided not to waste time peering behind every bush and tree for Bracken. If he had come in that direction at all, he was most certainly making his way to the fields, the scene of his recent blissful contentment. There was, of course, always the possibility that he might come trotting towards us in the belief that three such exotic travellers might be bearing gifts of oats, pony nuts or maize. He had, after all, a far distant cousin who had known of such things.

Such fanciful whimsies however could not dispel the over-riding gloom of our normally friendly little wood. Beneath our feet the path oozed mud and slime, and the ghosts of brambles past snatched at our unwary ankles. Every tree seemed to be bending downwards dripping rain-tears of some great primeval grief.

A solitary cock-pheasant, his splendid hues dimmed like an Old Master painting, trailed his once glorious tail feathers in the mud, too disconsolate to fly. A fallen tree-trunk lay dank and glistening like a wounded, dying beast.

'The woods decay, the woods decay and fall,' I quoted quietly to myself.

'The vapours weep their burthen to the ground,' intoned a voice from under the monk's cowl.

I stopped abruptly, and my stick lost three of its inches as, for the umpteenth time, it sank in the mud.

'Tennyson, I believe,' said Mr Thompson. 'Oh yes,' he added, and a sudden twinkle in his eyes lit up his gold spectacles and the shadowy grotto of his hood. 'It wasn't *all* maths and economics, you know.'

We plodded, slithered and squelched our way on. Funny, I thought, I had never imagined a bank manager reading anything but Statements and the *Financial Times*. Poetry and petty cash seemed to have little in common – unless it was the alliteration.

I wondered what sort of poet a bank manager would actually prefer. A good, solid respectable sort, of course, with his feet set firmly in his regular blank verse. Who else but Wordsworth? Who else could write:

'The world is too much with us; late and soon,
Getting and spending, we lay waste our lives.'?

Ah well, we had done our share of spending as Mr Thompson's very presence proved. But whether we would be getting anything out of it was another matter. Bracken had seen to that.

'I think he's here!' George's triumphant cry cut across my thoughts. We had reached the edge of the wood and the open field lay ahead of us.

Several four-legged blobs were scattered across it in varying shades of brown, black and grey, with the occasional bright green New Zealand rug hiding its smug wearer. I checked shapes, colours and names on my fingers, but Bracken was not among them.

'Now what?' asked Mr Thompson, and I sensed his enthusiasm had dampened somewhat like the edges of his once immaculate shirt cuffs as he wiped a droplet from his nose.

'We'll just take a look in the next field,' said George wearily. 'It leads directly into the lane. We can walk straight back the shortest way, and phone the police.'

The next field presented the blankest landscape I had ever seen. Flat and low-lying it wore a veil of grey chiffon-like drizzle which muted and smothered every vestige of colour. We knew at a glance that even the wiliest native pony could not disguise his flesh and blood presence against the skeletal branches of the surrounding trees and hedges. The whole scene had a strange, brooding unearthly atmosphere like an empty stage-set awaiting a performance of the witches' scene from *Macbeth*.

Suddenly, a strident streak of sound pierced the misty drizzle and echoed eerily in the woods behind. It was repeated, this time with a ghostly musical back-up group of haunting, yapping howls.

'Wh-what on earth was that?' whispered Mr Thompson, his hood slipping backwards to reveal his startled face.

'That', explained George, suddenly rigid with attention, was a sound unfamiliar to his city ears but well-known to ours – the local hunt in full cry.

He gave our visibly shaken guest a long searching look, then turned and studied me, leaning more heavily than usual on my stick.

'I think it's time we gave up and went back,' he said. 'We all need something to eat.'

It was at that point that I met my old arch-enemy, the gate: our first encounter since that fateful day.

Chained to a post for its sins, it leaned disconsolately at an angle. Drizzle accumulated on its upper bar and ran tearfully down its weather beaten frame. Could it be that it was actually sorry for what it had done?

I gave myself a mental shake; I was getting fanciful, what with eerie mists and remembered pain.

'You've got the keys, haven't you, George?' I asked briskly. George unlocked the rusty padlock and pushed the gate slowly open. It gave out a low, appealing moan, but I limped through with my head in the air. It wasn't going to get off as easily as that!

As we entered our drive for the third time that day, a totally unexpected sight met us. Posed against the winter jasmine as if from the pages of *Country Life*, an elegant rider, his hunting pink soaked to a sort of stewed plum, sat astride what could only be described as a Truly Splendid Steed. Beside him, held unbelievably by a single strand of bright orange bale string was a four-legged, mud plastered hearthrug.

'I believe this is yours,' he said in unmistakable Joint-Master accents. 'Tagged on a few miles back. Grand little chap. Up front all the way. Thought I'd better bring him back though. Getting in the way a bit – no offence of course. Can't stay long.

Promised to catch up as soon as possible.'

He leaned over and handed the astonished George the bale string.

'Good day to you,' he said, raising an elegant whip in salute, and he was gone in a clatter of well-shod hooves.

As if struck dumb, all three of us looked at Bracken, and Bracken looked at us. Beneath the dripping rat's tail forelock, the brown eyes gleamed with quietly contented triumph. As George led him back to the small front paddock, a half remembered conversation glimmered back into my mind.

'He's a super jumper,' his last owner had said, 'and he simply *adores* hunting. He'll go first or last any time.'

There was no doubt about it. Our grand little chap had galloped the full length of the small paddock to gain momentum and cleared a five-foot fence in answer to a distant huntsman's horn.

'Well,' said Mr Thompson, breaking the spell, 'I'd better be getting along.'

I looked at my watch appalled; it was exactly twenty-seven minutes to the departure of his train.

'But you can't go without *something* inside you,' I gasped. 'George!' I yelled frantically, 'Help Mr Thompson out of those wet things, and I'll put the kettle on.'

In the kitchen, Mrs B's meticulously timed meal was now a burnt offering to the capricious gods.

Speeding back to the station Mr Thompson took appreciative sips of his instant coffee (served in a mug in case it slopped) and munched his way through three digestive biscuits. We reached the platform just as the signals showed green.

Miserably I handed him the envelope containing Bracken's photographs.

'I thought you might like to see what he *normally* looks like,' I said faintly.

'Ah, good idea,' he said, putting it straight into his pocket without a glance. 'I'll – er – study them in depth in the train.'

Back in his city-cut overcoat he was very much the visiting bank manager again.

'Thank you for a most interesting visit,' he added with a courteous Coutts bow, Type Three. 'It isn't often one gets the chance to see the – er – real countryside,' and he stepped up into the compartment with only the faintest of mud-rings showing where the edge of George's gumboots had been.

As the train pulled out of the station, his face re-appeared briefly at the window, a biscuit crumb still clinging to his upper lip.

'Over five feet did you say?'

We were still nodding dumbly as the last carriage vanished round the bend.

Later that evening, I succumbed to 'one of my off-spells'. These invariably followed a period when I had been doing too much for too long, ignoring the danger signs. The symptoms were a nagging, grating pain down my right side, and a feeling of exhaustion close to collapse. I fell sound asleep on the settee before the dying fire.

I was awakened some centuries later by the insistent ringing of the telephone.

'I'll get it,' rang out George's voice from the kitchen on a waft of frying fish fingers.

'Five-one-three-four? Yes? Oh, how good of you to call . . . Not at all, it was our pleasure. We were only sorry that everything got so muddled . . . She's fine, a bit tired but she's had a little nap . . .'

There followed an incredibly long silence. I craned my neck and could just see George's right ear and his knuckles clenched, unnaturally white, round the receiver.

When he spoke again I detected the very slightest of tremors.

'Yes, good aren't they? It's an old camera but it never lets us down . . . Of course! If she's having riding lessons there's no difficulty . . . Yes, a grand little chap . . . oh absolutely . . . completely reliable, knows his job . . . A what? . . . a birthday present? Lucky little girl! We can attach a birthday card if you like – you can rely on my wife's good taste . . . I beg your pardon? . . . Harness? . . . I – er – think you mean "tack" Mr Thompson . . . But of course, no problem, it's been well used of course, but still in excellent condition . . . Then shall we say another one-fifty? That's less than we paid for the saddle itself . . . That's right . . . eight-fifty altogether . . . I beg your pardon? . . . Oh, just put it through the – er – usual channels and lop it off the overdraft.

'What about transport? – Oh, you have? Good! A shared load is always cheaper. We look forward to seeing you about eleven on Saturday then, and we'll have him ready and waiting . . . Not at all . . . yes, I'll tell her . . . Thank you for ringing. Goodbye.'

For the second time that day George stood dramatically in the doorway. There was a quietly triumphant expression in his eyes that I had seen before – in Bracken's.

'Find that corkscrew, Peg-leg,' he said, ruffling my hair with a sudden tenderness. 'We've got something to celebrate!'

3 · Damp Squib

'Is *this* the one?' the young man's eyes, already considerably magnified by his thick-lensed spectacles, looked enormous with wonder. In fact, everything about him seemed enormous. Well over six feet in height with broad shoulders and a thick thatch of wavy brown hair he looked more like a professional rugby player than the nine-to-five penpusher I knew him to be. Only the spectacles and the first signs of stooping shoulders betrayed that he was destined to be a weekend rider.

'He's a beaut,' he breathed, hardly the wisest of first observations for one who might shortly be discussing price.

'I told you it would be worth a try,' said his diminutive wife, who scarcely reached his chest. She was pink with pleasure at his obvious surprise and rubbed a neat little blonde head against his sleeve, puppy-dog fashion.

'Yes, he's a handsome chap, isn't he?' I said, and could have bitten my tongue off for the mistake. The young man's face flushed scarlet and he seemed to find an urgent need to adjust his hard hat.

'Er – yes,' he said.

The junior insurance agent's reaction to The Squire had given me a curious sensation of a recurring dream. I understood only too well. It was less than two years since George and I had been in exactly the same position.

The advertisement had been innocuous and ordinary. The horse for sale was a grey 16.2 hands gelding of good temperament, suitable for novice or experienced rider. The one mark of distinction was that it was 'registered at Weatherby's'. Like the advertisement, the price was unexceptional, and our reason for going to see the animal was chiefly that it was only a few miles away.

The address proved to be a somewhat exclusive one, the block of loose boxes behind it brick built and immaculate. There were signs of top class professionalism everywhere: the new bale of clean straw at each door, stable rugs airing on a high rail, the headcollars with coiled lead reins at each window sill (with a spare one 'for emergency use only') the fire extinguisher prominently placed, and not a sign of a muck heap or a single fly anywhere.

We identified ourselves to a stable lad whose grey forelock and weather-beaten face made nonsense of the traditional title. He nodded, touched his cap and disappeared into the second box.

We were totally unprepared for the vision he brought out.

'Is this the horse advertised?' asked George openly astonished.

'It's 'imself, sorr.' The bluest eyes I've ever seen studied us keenly from under the cloth cap.

There are many interpretations of the word 'grey' in the horse world. It can vary from a dingy nondescript off-white to a murky dark pewter. This one was an unusual gun-metal shade with a faint dappling of silver on the back and quarters. All four elegant legs were jet black as were the mane and tail. And over all, a gleaming irridescent sheen which made him appear to have been cast out of some rare and exquisite metal and burnished to the ultimate satisfaction of a consummate artist.

He was unmistakably a thoroughbred, from the proud arch of the muscled neck and the small head to the slender but powerful legs. Held by his tiny Irish groom – an ex-jockey if ever there was one – he stood completely still but alert.

George fumbled in his pocket and produced a scrap of paper.

'*This* advert?' he said, still incredulous.

The groom casually looped the reins over one elbow and produced spectacles from his breast pocket to study the wording.

'That's right, sorr. Is it yourself or the lady wants to try 'im?'

George took a noticeable step backwards.

'Er, I'm not a rider, my wife is,' he mumbled.

I gulped and cursed myself for coming on an impulse without Rosemary's support.

'I – er – he's rather big,' I said, then felt a complete idiot; the size had been clearly stated in the advertisement.

The bright blue eyes watched me closely.

'There's the schoolin' area,' he said, jerking a thumb over his shoulder. 'Fenced in,' he added pointedly.

I felt better. 'All right,' I said, hoping that my voice was not as wobbly as my knees.

' 'Tis Pat's me name,' the stable lad volunteered, 'Sure an' he's a kind fella, this one,' and I sensed he was trying to put me at my ease. Certainly the 'kind' helped a lot.

'You'll be needin' a mountin' block,' said Pat in matter-of-fact tones and led the gelding towards a low, ornamental wall.

This time I really was relieved. We had actually come just to *look* at the animal with some of our more experienced students in mind; I had never really imagined I would ride it on first sight, and now, underneath the general apprehension had been the nervous thought – would I have to be legged-up in true jockey fashion?

With the courtesy of a bygone age, Pat offered a hand to help me on to the low brickwork then gently steered me up and into the saddle. The grey turned limpid eyes to study my left toe as if surprised that a female of the species was on his back, then looked steadily forward again, ears erect.

Pat adjusted the girth and stirrups with meticulous care, handed me a leather-bound riding crop with a slight bow and stood back respectfully. Suddenly, I felt like a duchess.

The slightest touch of my heels and we were away on a brisk, measured walk, each stride of the long legs seeming to cover an extraordinary distance. We went twice round the arena in no time – no thoroughbred tantrums, no high-spirited impatience, just a quiet acceptance of my authority. George and Pat leaned over the post-and-rail fencing, one looking anxious, the other quizzical.

'Right, madam,' I said briskly to myself. 'Don't let the side down. Get on with it!'

The merest shortening of the reins, the merest hint of the heels and we were trotting. It took several minutes for me to adjust to the incredible length of the stride. At the 'rise' I felt suspended in mid-air like Nijinsky and we were no sooner at one end of the arena than it was time to loop back to the other.

It was a curiously exhilarating experience, this sensation of power, speed and elegance obeying without question my slightest touch. I felt the tension leave my body, and I turned to give George a reassuring smile. To my astonishment there were now three figures leaning over the rail.

'It's Mr O'Connor!' yelled George as we sailed past, then as I changed rein and came round again, 'The OWNER!'

I nodded, feeling rather superior in my new-found confidence, seated as I was, so elegantly above their heads.

'Come on, handsome,' I said as one silken ear swivelled back to listen. 'Let's show the gallery what we can do.'

The canter was definitely not a success. The big gelding stretched out his neck and argued with the bit when I tried to collect him in. The speed was unbelievable and it was clear that he was frustrated by the confined space.

If there had been enough room to gather momentum I felt

sure he would have cleared the fence. There was something oddly disunited about his gait, too. Or was it just that he simply never got the chance to get into rhythm in the restricted space?

Feeling somewhat deflated after my show of pride, I reined in level with the three figures (no trouble with his brakes, I noted).

Pat was instantly at my side, and with the same old-fashioned courtesy, discreetly helped me to dismount, ran up the stirrups, and with a nod to his boss, led the horse away.

George made the necessary introductions.

'You handled him very well,' said Mr O'Connor. His accent was unmistakably Irish, but unlike Pat's it had been well ironed out in some exclusive English school. Crinkly grey eyes smiled at me from a lined face tanned almost to mahogany beneath a swathe of incongruously pure white hair.

'There was something a bit – well – odd about his canter,' I said. 'Was it just the confined space?'

Mr O'Connor beamed engagingly. 'Could be your seat. No offence, of course,' he said, 'but he's used to a more forward position.'

Incredibly the full significance of this remark did not at first sink in.

'He has such a long stride,' I said. 'He obviously doesn't like being hemmed in. I thought at one point he was going to try and clear the fence.'

'Does he jump?' asked George.

Mr O'Connor gave him a long, steady look. 'He's a chaser,' he said, adding glumly, 'or *was*.'

There were several seconds of silence. Everything was beginning to fall into place. The 'registered at Weatherby's' bit should have warned us.

'Then why is he for sale at such a – well – reasonable price? He's a stunner, and so well mannered,' said the mystified George.

'Seems to have lost his gumption,' sighed Mr O'Connor carefully lighting a cheroot. 'He's had three firsts and been placed umpteen times, then suddenly started fizzling out on the home stretch. Doesn't even try any more,' and he blew a mournful smoke-ring heavenwards.

'Perhaps you've overworked him and he's just gone stale,' I ventured. 'Maybe he just needs a rest.'

Mr O'Connor studied his well polished boots. 'Haven't got time or money to waste on rest cures for neurotics,' he said. 'Anyway, I've got some young stock coming over from Ireland and I need his box. That's why he's cheap.'

'Excuse us while we have a little chat,' said George, and Mr O'Connor moved politely away to stroke a wandering lurcher.

'What d'you think?' he whispered. 'You've been on his back.'

I felt confused and uncertain. 'I don't know *what* to think,' I whispered back. 'I'm not sure about his canter. It's all right, I suppose, but it's *peculiar* somehow. And why is a thoroughbred like that *really* so cheap? Do you think he's telling the truth? And yet . . . and yet . . .'

I was remembering the sheer exhilaration of that long, willing stride, and the tremendous boost to my ego as I sat on the gleaming back.

Already I could see myself trotting nonchalantly through the village in immaculate hacking jacket, skirting the parked Jaguars and nodding charmingly (but with a certain aloofness) to the faces peering round the delphiniums from above the Laura Ashley smocks.

Ours was rapidly becoming a dormitory village for well-heeled commuters. Decrepit old barns had been converted into desirable residences with the inevitable exposed beams. Grass verges were manicured to velvet smoothness, and woe betide any country animal, horse, dog, cow or sheep, that dared to set hoof or paw on it; or, worse still, the unthinkable, leave its visiting card. Ye old carriage lamps lit up the rambling roses artistically arranged round the newly antiqued rustic doors, and professionally landscaped cottage gardens matched the Sanderson's prints.

Sooner or later someone was bound to remark, 'Isn't that a thoroughbred she's riding?' and they would sniff and clip too much off the hedge with their Wilkinson's Blade shears.

George's voice broke into my thoughts.

'We'll let the vet decide,' he said, suddenly practical. 'Mr O'Connor!' he called, 'We'll have him – subject to a vet's certificate.'

There was the briefest flicker of relief behind the crinkles. 'Good,' he said, 'You arrange it, and – er – which one will it be?

Our vet's examination was painstaking and thorough and took the best part of two hours. Eyes and legs were studied minutely. Heart and wind were checked after Pat had galloped the full length of a nearby field with a thunder of hooves that made the hairs on my neck tingle. I might be apprehensive about his canter, but there was certainly nothing wrong with his gallop. Was I mad to be contemplating such a horse? Considerable time was spent in close inspection of the feet. The hind hooves had an unusually flattened shape at the front, but were otherwise as sound as the fore.

The vet finally wiped his brow and filled in the certificate on the spot. It recorded that the only faults he could find were a small wart on the offside stifle, and the fact that the animal needed the attention of the farrier. We also learned for the first time that the gelding was called The Squire, that he was seven-eighths thoroughbred and that he had been sired by a famous racing name that even I recognised.

George and Mr O'Connor shook hands. 'I'll have the cash waiting for you when you deliver him tomorrow,' said George.

Mr O'Connor seemed not a little relieved that all had gone so smoothly.

'I'll miss old Squib,' he said.

'Squib?' said George.

'Yes, the lads generally called him that. At least it was Damp Squib,' and he grinned ruefully.

'That's terrible,' I said. 'A superb animal like that! He's going to have his full title from now on. The Squire – and nothing else.'

When The Squire arrived it seemed the entire village turned out to gaze with supercilious wonder at the elaborate, gleaming horsebox. Fitted with all mod. con. for both human and equine passengers it looked slick and incongruous in the calculated olde worlde charm.

George and I, with Rosemary and our two remaining working pupils, lined up respectfully to receive him, like a Victorian household.

Pat led him out.

'Oh-h-h,' said Rosemary.

'Oo-oo-o,' breathed the girls in unison.

'Mm-m-m,' murmured George.

I was merely speechless.

Pat had excelled himself; the polished silvery flanks gleamed with a mirror-like sheen, and the black mane and tail were shot with a myriad irridescent glints. The Squire walked down the ramp with the poise of a dancer, each elegant hoof placed delicately and unerringly. The small, alert ears pricked forward as he inspected us; the eyes were large and kind, but strangely sad.

'His b-box is waiting,' spluttered Rosemary and rushed to open the door as if for royalty.

The next morning a rather tense Rosemary knocked on the kitchen door as we were beheading our boiled eggs.

'Could you spare a moment?' she asked.

'We're just having breakfast,' I said. 'Is it urgent?'

'No – well, yes – er, no. You'd better finish your breakfast first. I'll be in the new horse's box.'

'That sounds a bit ominous,' murmured George as we both ignored the toast and marmalade and dashed out.

We were several yards away from Box 4 when a strange odour insinuated itself into my nostrils. They say the olfactory sense is the quickest to revive near-forgotten memories. The smell was distinctly zoological, transporting me back to a childhood visit to Chessington, but which species was responsible I could not recall.

The sight that met our eyes in Box 4 was incredible. The clean straw placed there only the previous evening was now a soggy, malodorous mess with no sign of the normal equine droppings. Long rivulets of glistening yellow ooze ran down the kick-boards and similar streaks marred the silvery hind quarters of the occupant. We reeled back as Rosemary staggered out looking pale green. The Squire gazed at us apologetically.

'It must be the change of diet,' said Rosemary gasping for air.

'What on earth did you give him?' I asked, searching frantically for a handkerchief.

Rosemary bridled. 'The same as all the others: horse nuts, bran, sugar-beet and dampened hay.'

'Any additives?'

'Yes, a spoonful of cod liver oil and a shake of mineral supplement.'

'Something doesn't agree with him,' mumbled George from behind a paper tissue. 'Probably the cod liver oil. Cut it out next time.'

'I can't just muck out as usual,' muttered Rosemary. 'I'll have to *hose* out, and he'll probably need a bath as well.'

There followed several weeks of dogged trial and error with different permutations of the entire contents of the feed store – even simple hay was omitted for a trial period – but all to no avail. Every feed we devised produced the same result. Deep in the orchestra pit of The Squire's stomach a Wagnerian overture would begin. Rising to a full scale grand opera, it would end in a fanfare of trumpet blasts of sulphurous fumes from the animal's rear, with a semi-liquid stream of what my biology teacher years before had delicately referred to as a semi-solid chyme.

Should any of his repertoire still be lingering when he was out exercising, the final crescendo would be accompanied by an upward flick of the hind feet – not a buck as such, merely a reflex action to the discomfort, but sudden enough to send the unwary rider half way up the animal's back.

Through it all, The Squire remained willing and docile, and oddly resigned.

'I can't imagine why he isn't edgy and bad-tempered with all that – er – wind rolling around his insides,' said George. 'Let's have one final try. Feed him on just plain nuts.'

'I know who's going to be plain nuts if this goes on much longer,' muttered Rosemary darkly. 'What did the vet say when you rang him? After all, he signed the certificate.'

'He said to – er – check his diet,' said George lamely, averting his gaze.

There still remained the additional question of the uneven canter. Walking and trotting all was well (no-one would risk a gallop with that flip of the heels) but at the canter the horse seemed unable to maintain the three-beat rhythm for any length of time.

'Perhaps his musical upbringing doesn't include waltz time,' suggested a cheerful student as, once again, we all noticed the hesitant missed beat.

Rosemary was not amused.

'You really shouldn't have gone without me,' she said. 'Didn't you notice *anything*?'

'Well, yes, I did,' I admitted feeling a fool, 'but . . .'

'I know, I know. He's a super-looker and so nice natured, but I can't help wondering about the people who sold him to you. How did they disguise this lot? Was he doped d'you suppose?'

I could only shake my head. I had already asked myself the same question a thousand times.

There was no shortage of helpful advice from knowledgeable friends. Could it be worms? We wormed him thoroughly, standing by to ensure that the last milligramme of the powder was consumed – no effect. Could it be bot fly larvae? ('They do *ghastly* things to the lining of the stomach, my dear.') But one of the symptoms of that problem was a capricious appetite. The Squire ate every concoction we devised with relish and appreciation. Had we ever thought of a chiropractor?

'A Cairo what?' I asked.

'A chiropractor. You know, a bit like an osteopath; they manipulate bones and things, the spine mostly.'

'On a HORSE *that* size?' I said incredulously. 'You have to be joking!'

'Oh no,' my friend was rummaging around in her shoulder-bag. 'They reckon all sorts of things arise from spinal problems, something to do with pressure I believe. I've got the phone number of one here if you want it. Let's face it, anything's worth a try,' and she held an embroidered handkerchief to her nose.

That evening I discussed it with George. His reaction was the same as mine.

'Everybody will think we're mad,' he said.

'They'll think we're madder if we put up with this much longer,' I groaned. 'One of these days when there's a strong wind blowing towards the village, the Residents' Association will send the sanitary inspector to our door. Let's ring the woman and have a chat.'

'A WOMAN!' shouted George. 'Now I know it's crazy. It'll need Muhammad Ali to manipulate *that*.'

The voice that answered was pleasant and businesslike.

'We wondered if you could give us some help with – er – a horse,' I said feebly.

'Yes?' she said.

'He's quite big. 16.2 hands.'

'Yes?' she said.

'Well, er, when could you call?' I gave her our address.

'Oh, that's easy,' she said, 'I'll be in your direction tomorrow if that's any good. It'll be about mid-day though. I've got a call to make before that,' and she mentioned the name of a well-known, highly respected stud.

'What are his symptoms?' she asked.

'Trouble with his – er – bowels,' I all but whispered.

'Ah,' she said. 'See you tomorrow then.'

I looked at George who was pretending to read the *Radio Times*.

'She's going to the stud first,' I said incredulously.

'I expect one of the grooms has got a slipped disc,' was the wry reply.

4 · The Squire

The next morning an immaculately clean box was prepared into which The Squire would be led the moment the car appeared.

'Have you ever worked with a chiropractor before?' I asked Rosemary, letting the term slip casually off my tongue as if I'd known it for years.

'No, but I'm looking forward to the experience,' she replied equally casually, and I suspected she had looked it up in the dictionary the night before when I rang to warn her of the day's preparations.

But what preparations? Would the lady arrive, white-coated, with a selection of mysterious and fearsome gadgets in the boot? Would she use some sort of tranquilliser? Ought I to have a good strong rope ready? (I put one in the tack room just in case.) And what about her fee? In my anxiety I had forgotten to mention this all-important subject. I placed several notes in my left pocket and my cheque-book in the right.

At 11.45 a.m. a battered mini came into the drive and a dumpy middle-aged figure stepped out. She wore knee-length boots, faded jeans and a quilted jacket which made her look like an advertisement for Michelin tyres. Light brown hair was dragged back into an incongruous pony-tail.

'Yes? Can I help you?' I asked politely. We were used to odd strangers losing their way in the cul-de-sac of our lane.

'I understand you've got a gelding with problems,' she said. 'Can you show me which one?'

'Y-yes, of course,' I mumbled, desperately trying to hide my surprise.

'Just a tick,' she said, and opened up the boot of the mini.

Here it comes, I thought; the white coat and the gadgetry and watched, wide-eyed, as she produced a bright blue milk crate.

'To stand on,' she explained cheerfully in answer to my raised brows.

We had wasted our time preparing the immaculate box; the patient was to be treated outside. She made no comment as we led him out, but studied the flattened fronts of his hind hooves with interest.

She removed her padded jacket to reveal an ample, matronly bosom under a bright pink blouse, rolled up her sleeves and placed the milk crate upside down at The Squire's nearside. For the first time since we had known him he looked apprehensive; blue milk crates and buxom females were not in his range of experience.

Rosemary held his head. I walked to the offside and stood, mystified, at a respectful distance. Our two working pupils gaped open mouthed from the empty box. There was total silence except for an anxious blowing of the nostrils by the patient.

I watched fascinated as two sets of plump fingers began to move along the horse's spine, 'walking' delicately like a pair of chubby spiders. No other part of their owner was visible.

'Mm-m-m,' came from the other side.

The fat spiders disappeared and suddenly the bases of two muscular palms struck simultaneously as if from nowhere.

There was a muffled crack and The Squire staggered sideways. I held my breath ready for the display of thoroughbred histrionics. None came. Unbelievably, the horse merely regained his balance and stood still.

There were sounds of the milk crate being repositioned, and again the plump spiders began their pilgrimage, this time gently and carefully up the neck. Again they disappeared and the muscular palms struck. A second muffled crack sent The Squire off balance but he showed no fear or resentment.

'Ex-chaser, is he?'

I could not believe my ears.

'Yes,' I gulped. 'How did you know?'

'Typical case,' she said. 'Had a bad fall at speed I should say. They usually get it here or here,' and an authoritative finger indicated a spot high up on the neck, the other at the loin. 'This poor chap's got the lot.'

Suddenly she disappeared and stood directly behind the tail, her ample bosom actually touching it – no small risk with an unfamiliar horse. But by now I had noticed a curious stillness about The Squire. We were used to his stoic acceptance of his problems, but this was a total tranquillity, an animal at peace.

Again silence fell, her audience mesmerised. Leaning with her chin practically on the dock she eyed the angle of each hip, then without warning took a single step sideways, knees braced, and brought the flat of her hand, with the full force of her shoulder and body, in a hard blow against the right hip. It was not so much the weight of the blow – The Squire was a lot of horse – but the unexpected angle which took us all by surprise. This time, The Squire grunted, shot several feet to the left, shook himself gently, then stood calmly at ease.

'That's it,' she said, wiping the sweat off her brow with her sleeve. 'He'll be a bit stiff for a few days, but let him walk about. Nothing strenuous for a week or so.'

She picked up her jacket and milk crate and started to walk back through the yard.

'Nice place you've got here,' she said conversationally.

'You're lucky. Just give me a ring if you have any problems, but I don't think you will.'

I was still trying to collect my wits.

'Wh – what about your fee?' I asked.

She pondered for a moment and adjusted the elastic band of her lop-sided pony-tail.

'Oh, I was in this direction anyway. A tenner will do if that's all right with you.'

I stood rooted to the spot, engulfed in exhaust fumes, long after the ancient mini had gone.

George was openly sceptical the next morning.

'Sounds like the ultimate con-trick to me,' he said. 'You can say goodbye to your tenner,' but I noticed we were both out in the yard a little earlier than usual.

The three girls were standing at Box 4 their heads motionless in the dark interior. That was unusual for a start.

Rosemary turned as we reached them.

'I just don't believe it,' she said in a hushed voice. 'I just don't believe it. Look at that!'

Five pairs of eyes solemnly studied that. It was a neat pyramid of perfectly formed spheres resting in a bed of clean, undisturbed straw. Artistically symmetrical, it resembled a brown version of one of those ornamental bowls of piled white china fruit so often seen in dining rooms.

'Do you think,' said George in awestruck tones, 'we ought to do a still life painting of it, and send it to the Tate?'

Further inspection supported our first impression. Other similar neatly-placed piles were to be found. Only one patch of wet straw was visible arranged discreetly it seemed on the farthest side. Mucking out would take a matter of minutes only. The Squire gazed at us serenely.

'Have you noticed,' said Linda, one of the girls, 'he seems to have a different kind of quietness about him now – not so, well, *resigned*.'

From that day onwards there were no more malodorous

orchestrations in Box 4. The Squire was the star of our establishment. News soon spread that we had that rare and priceless creature – a powerful, beautiful thoroughbred with the placid nature of a family pony. Rosemary and the girls set about a carefully planned programme of exercising and schooling, and it was not long before the very last hint of the uneven canter had gone, and the pained flick of the heels was soon a memory. Only the impatience with the confined space of the manège remained, the long legs covering it contemptuously but obediently in seconds.

Out in the open fields he came into his own. He would thunder down the full stretch quite literally taking his rider's breath away. Yet the gentlest request with the hands and he would come quietly to a smooth stop.

Several sets of cross-country jumps were arranged along one side of the middle field. These were his delight and joy. With ears pricked in anticipation, he took them all in his stride, accurately gauging the point of take off, elevation and landing spot. The rider was merely a privileged passenger on his back.

Needless to say, everyone wanted to ride The Squire. Non-jumpers jumped fearlessly with sparkling eyes, and those who had never galloped in their lives went home to bore family and friends with endless tales of their prowess and speed.

'Don't you think we ought to ring up the chiropractor lady and thank her?' I said to George one day.

'Might be a good idea,' he replied a trifle grudgingly. 'But I still wonder whether it was just a fluke of timing.'

I rang and gave her a glowing description of the situation.

'Good,' she said in matter-of-fact tones, and managed to convey in that single syllable that, much as she liked to hear from grateful clients, she was *rather* busy and couldn't spare much time to talk about routine matters. 'It's only a case of relieving nerve pressure,' she said, as if that explained it all. 'Thank you for ringing. You know where I am if you need me again.'

There are many phrases in the English language which have lost their original meaning through over-use. The statement 'I shall never forget the day when . . .' is all too often a mere introduction to the re-telling of some worn out anecdote. But I truly shall never forget the day I first rode The Squire out alone into the open countryside.

It had been a singularly trying February, with sharp winds, snow, sleet and the occasional icy fog. Then on March 1st, as if the weather, like the calendar, had turned over a new leaf, a crisp bright sunshine bathed the countryside in a near-forgotten clarity of tingling light. Underfoot the ground was still hard but not icy, and The Squire and I stepped out smartly to explore the beginnings of a new Spring.

To my surprise, the winter blanketings had obscured a surge of activity in the hedgerows and fields. As if summoned by the magic wand of the sun's ray, bright celandines, pink-tipped daisies and even the occasional pale violet, already glowed in the stubby grass, and here and there, a half opened daffodil stood up defiantly declaring that, yes, Spring was definitely on its way. The willows by the stream were already wearing their silky white pom-poms and the early hazel catkins waved to us shyly as we passed.

Turning into the middle field, I felt a tremor of anticipation run through The Squire's limbs – the cross-country jumps lay ahead. There had been a considerable change in him since our first meeting. Although willing as always, he had lost that curious air of resignation which I had originally interpreted as mere obedience. He had a new sparkle, a new alert interest, and the ability to gauge and respond to his rider's mood without ever taking advantage of his speed and strength.

I leaned forward slightly and gave him his head; he did the rest. This, I thought, all but intoxicated by the rush of clean, cold air, and the confident soaring upwards – to the very heavens it sometimes seemed – must be the nearest thing to flying. 'A privacy of glorious light is thine,' Wordsworth once said of the skylark. The Squire and I shared something very similar on that bright March day.

At the far edge of the field a lone figure watched our exhilaration, leaning inwards over the low fence from the farmland beyond. It was old Mr Fred, so named to distinguish him from his two brothers, Robert and Arthur. The three farmers, known collectively as the Beresford Brothers, had moved down from their native North in the depression to find new pastures, literally, for their sheep. Now all three, well past their three-score years and ten, and clad in ancient tweeds and even more ancient moleskins, were respected, feared or loved according to the age range of their critics.

'Nice day,' said Mr Fred, tapping out his pipe. 'That be a good 'un you've got there.'

'Yes,' I said, tingling with pride and fresh air. 'How are things with you?'

'T'sun's bringin' 'em out.' He grinned toothlessly at his own little joke and jerked his cloth cap towards the field behind him.

Several wobbly bundles of white wool with black faces were skipping about by the placid ewes.

'Twins,' he said, indicating the smallest pair fighting for their mother's teats, tiny tails wagging ecstatically. 'T'auld ewe allus gives me a good pair.'

The Squire and I leaned over the fence and watched the scene. In that clear March sun, the white wool seemed exceptionally so against the sprouting greenery, even whiter than the last skeins of snow which still lingered in the shadowed part of a hedge.

'You know, Mr Fred,' I confided, 'All my life I've wanted to cuddle a newborn lamb, but never seem to have had the chance.'

Mr Fred did not bother to reply. With the easy action of a lifetime's experience, he picked up a tiny, woolly bundle, and stretching out scrawny arms, offered it to The Squire to inspect, nostrils twitching, then handed it up to me. Neither animal seemed remotely surprised at this gentle action, and soon the little black face was nestled, infant like, in the curve of my neck. The Squire, reins loosely knotted over his neck, quietly investigated the sprouting grass.

Mr Fred re-lit his pipe and leaned contentedly on the wooden rail to survey his increasing flock. I sat in the fragrance of his tobacco and cradled the tiny scrap of trusting warmth. It was a few precious moments of total peace, and yet it was all eternity. I wondered how many people would ever be as privileged as I to share the silent companionship of powerful beauty, work-worn wisdom and new-born innocence, at one and the same time, and on such a perfect day.

I did not know then, as I do now, that it was the last time Mr Fred would cherish one of t'auld ewe's twins.

It was the memory of this day that was uppermost in my mind, when, after a disconcerting visit to the physiotherapist, I was obliged to face the facts about the future of our horses.

'We'll have to advertise,' said George, 'Potential "good owners" don't just happen along.'

'But how do we find out who *is* a good owner?' I wailed, 'Even supposing we get any replies.'

'I'll find out,' said George, and he meant it.

The advertising section of the *Horse and Hound* was a daunting sight. Page after page of 'display, semi-display and classified' listed seemingly perfect horses, and yet there was a depressing similarity in the wording.

'Supposing we start with The Squire,' said George, avoiding my eyes. 'We can't just say "Grey gelding, 16.2 hands. Good novice or experienced ride", and so on. It doesn't mean a thing. It sounds like umpteen other horses on the same page.'

'No, look at the shock *we* got,' I said, and we both smiled at the memory.

'Which reminds me,' said George casually, 'What do you think he was *really* worth, if they had known how simple the – er – cure was?'

'At least twice as much as we paid,' I answered absently.

'Good. Then that's settled,' said George.

'George, you can't!'

'Why not? We've sorted him out so we should get the benefit. Look at him now – thoroughbred performance without thoroughbred problems. Better horse – better price. Come on, you've got a way with words. Think up something different!'

I looked at the endless columns of repeated phrases and suddenly it was a challenge.

'How about "Handsome horse seeks handsome owner to share future successes" plus general details, then "genuine reason for sale"? It might work.'

It did. By nine p.m. on the date of issue we had received six telephone calls. They varied from the rapid-fire inquisition to a hesitant, nervy whisper. Curiously, it was this last which held my attention most completely.

'I can tell from your phone number that you are fairly near. Can we come over and try your horse?' The voice was light, breathy and very feminine.

'He's quite a powerful animal,' I said. 'He's really . . .' The near-whisper interrupted me.

'It's not for me, it's for my husband. He – er – doesn't know I'm ringing. He's very interested, but it's – er – your advertisement – the "handsome" bit, you know. He's a bit embarrassed. He – er – well, wears glasses.'

I warmed to the speaker. 'If it's any consolation, so do I,' I said, 'And I've ridden this horse.'

'Oh,' the shy voice gained confidence. 'He's very tall, actually, over six feet. But it's the firm's Riding Club. They're an Insurance Company,' she added conspiratorially as if this would explain everything. 'They are all such good riders and Adrian – er – my husband, is not much more than a beginner really, and he needs something that – well – knows more than he does, but – er – won't play him up in front of the others. But he doesn't just want a safe cob. Do you know what I mean?'

I knew exactly what she meant, and suddenly my own voice was husky with the ache in my throat.

'I think you'd better come over,' I said. 'This could be the horse for him. And it's not sales talk.'

Their joint reaction to The Squire was exactly as I anticipated. The hefty, bespectacled Adrian seemed to take on a new dignity of stature as he sat in the saddle. His tiny wife, 'Call me Anne', was speechless with admiration at the sight. The pair trotted effortlessly round the manège then broke into a steady, even canter. Horse and rider were perfectly at ease.

'He's just learning to jump,' confided Anne. 'Can this horse jump?'

'Oh yes,' I said, 'very well,' and resolved to keep The Squire's secret for the time being.

Even as I spoke, Anne caught her breath. The pair had turned sharply and cantered down the centre of the arena. A wide, coloured jump was directly in their path.

'Oh no! He's *not* going to try to jump!' gasped Anne and buried her face against my shoulder.

'Lean forward, Adrian, lean forward,' I breathed, and to this day, do not know whether I spoke the words aloud or not.

The Squire and his passenger cleared the pole effortlessly and without fuss. Adrian's bulk was still perfectly balanced as they came past.

'Did you see that, darling?' he cried ecstatically, 'I *jumped*!' Then, as he came round a second time, 'Watch me – I'm going to do it again!'

This time Anne watched, one slender hand clasped to her throat, baby-blue eyes like saucers.

Again they cleared the centre jump with inches to spare, and took in a pair of crossed poles on the way back.

As Adrian dismounted, I thought his tiny wife would explode with pride and excitement.

'Do you want to discuss it darling?' she breathed.

'Nothing to discuss,' replied Adrian, running unexpectedly knowledgeable fingers down the faultless tendons. 'I want this horse.'

'Some other people have made appointments . . .' I began.

'I'll nip straight back and get a deposit,' he interrupted. 'Is the holiday money still in the wardrobe?' he asked his wife.

She nodded, delighted with the success of her plan.

'Right,' he said, 'I'll have three hundred pounds back here within the hour. I'll bring the balance in cash tomorrow morning.'

I gulped, remembering George's insistence on the double figure, and my own doubts.

'D-don't you want him vetted? Most people do.' He was, after all, an insurance agent I reminded myself.

'Haven't you had him done?' he asked.

'Well, yes, but it was nearly two years ago. He's been as fit as a fiddle ever since.'

'That'll do fine.' He eased his spectacles up his nose. 'Come on, darling – home and back in an hour.'

As they were about to start the car there was a muffled conversation.

Aha! I thought, here come the 'ifs' and 'buts'.

But Adrian's head only popped out momentarily.

'I don't suppose you would sell his tack exactly as it stands, would you? Just add it to the total.'

Fifty-five minutes later they were back, and three hundred pounds in crisp notes lay beside the remains of my lunch on the kitchen table.

Over supper George and I discussed the staggering speed of events. George had a distinct 'I told you so' look about the price.

'Have you checked up on stabling and so on? They do realise he's a thoroughbred and can't just be kept in a field?'

I confessed that I hadn't had time to think about it.

'There's *still* time,' said George. 'You know the address. I'll get the car.'

In the gathering twilight their home looked unpretentious but neat, and was situated at the junction of a main road and narrow lane. We turned into the lane and saw at the end of the long, narrow garden, a brand new loose box with feed room attached. It was empty, and obviously lovingly prepared for an incoming V.I.P. Behind it, a wide gate led out into open country.

The following day George stayed at home 'in case there were any hitches' and I became adept at fending off other enquirers without putting them off altogether.

Adrian and Anne arrived with a borrowed horse-box, the balance in cash and 'some spare' to pay for the tack.

I felt a sharp tingling behind the eyes as The Squire walked willingly up the ramp with the same careful elegance as he had walked down nearly two years before, but under such different circumstances.

George went round to the driver's seat of the Land Rover and handed Adrian the receipt with an additional slip of paper.

'Those are the details of his breeding,' he said, 'in case you want to check him up at Weatherby's. I don't think you realise it,' he added casually, 'but you've just acquired an Irish chaser, and a successful one at that.'

Adrian's expression behind the thick lenses defied description.

'Really?' he gasped, and turned to Anne as her eyes met mine. 'Just wait till I tell the Riding Club THAT!'

Several weeks later we received a beautiful coloured photograph. It showed Adrian in the saddle, minus his glasses for better photogenic effect, and splendidly attired in a Swaine Adeney hacking jacket which exactly matched The Squire's subtle hues. A large rosette was prominently attached to the head-band.

On the back of the photograph was written in neat schoolgirlish handwriting 'Herewith the first of the "future successes". Don't they make a handsome pair? Love – and thank you, Anne.'

5 · Patchy

We had first heard about Patchy through the friend of a friend. Patchy's real name was Apache but scores of children, untroubled by the fetters of spelling or phonetics, had settled for Patchy. And who was to say they were wrong? For that was exactly what he was. A remarkable conglomeration of black, brown and white patterns vied with each other for supremacy, the whole effect seeming to obliterate his outline altogether. Which was perhaps just as well, for Patchy's lineage was as confused and uncertain as his colouring.

But whatever his visual oddities, Patchy was the darling of the local Riding for the Disabled Group. Small fingers traced the outlines of his geometric shapes that all too often eyes could not see, to the mystification of many a disbelieving observer. He knew that a dragged mane or a pulled tail meant only one thing – that uncertain little fists were learning in their fumbling way to grip and hold on.

Every nuance of childish utterance was familiar to his ears, from the whoop of glee to the whimper of uncertainty, and he would adjust his pace and movements accordingly, sometimes slowing to a gentle stop when the tears began to flow. He knew, too, the importance of standing completely still. What better than a solidly placed near-fore, with its firm grip of feathered fetlock, to encourage shaky hands to grasp and pull upwards till wobbly legs took their stand?

Let nervous females dither with their anxiety; he would never betray the childish trust of weak, ill-formed little bodies thrust against the warmth of his comforting bulk. Other ponies, he had heard, were ignorant of such matters, but he, Patchy, knew his job – and loved it.

One day, however, disaster struck in the form of a renegade muck trolley. The youthful driver of the small tractor that pulled it, misjudged a corner and caught Patchy's offside hock with the metal edge as it jack-knifed round. Patchy, who had been waiting patiently for his next little jockey to arrive in his wheelchair was led away, limping badly and leaving a trail of blood.

The injury was unsightly but not serious. Patchy was taken to a meadow to 'rest and let nature take its course'.

Alone and deprived of his little companions he called and called, but no-one came. Then, like many a human before him, he sought solace in food.

Months later when his girth was vastly expanded and the blemish had taken its place in the general mêlée of his patterns, his owner approached the friend of our friend. Did she know anyone who wanted a well-schooled pony and could give it the regular exercise it needed? She herself simply hadn't the time. So Patchy joined our ménage, and took his daily place in the manège.

As always he was an instant success with the less able and more nervous young riders, but gradually, first Rosemary then others, began to notice signs of a curiously split personality. Patchy's long, unexpected spell of the good life had left its mark. He seemed to be two different animals.

Under the saddle he was the perfect 'schoolmaster' pony, looking after his rider and responding to the aids with willingness and accuracy. Without it, he now lived by one maxim alone. The grass *was* greener on the other side of the fence, hedge, ditch or gate, and woe betide anything that stood between him and it. As one nervous girl remarked, the moment the bridle was off, the hunt was on.

My own accident and the ensuing change of circumstances meant that for the second time in his life, Patchy was left riderless. There was scarcely a day that George did not trudge wearily across the paddocks with hammer and nails to mend broken fences or trailing wires, despite our excellent meadow grass.

Even the telephone began to have uneasy connotations. Irate neighbours regularly listed the things he had broken through, smashed down, scrambled over, crawled under or squeezed past.

One day, George came in scarlet with anger and clutching his leg.

'That's *it*,' he muttered through clenched teeth. 'That animal will *have to go*!'

He rolled up his trouser leg to reveal a hideously multi-coloured bruise. Patchy had made a new discovery, probably genuinely by accident, that adult human shins could be disposed of in much the same way as gate posts. What was more, secure in this new-found knowledge, he had devised and refined his own little trick: if he trotted forward suddenly on the leading rein, his handler would be briefly left behind, level with his rump. A quick flick of the nearside hind and he could be free to enjoy all that glorious, glorious grass.

'I said he'll simply *have to go*,' George repeated himself tersely, applying a liberal slosh of 'Radiol: For Veterinary use only' to his swelling leg. 'With no-one to ride him he can only get worse. He needs work, and plenty of it!'

'But how on earth could we describe him to a potential buyer?' I asked. 'He's the perfect pony under saddle and . . .'

'. . . the perfect little demon without it,' finished George. 'We'll have to advertise him. We'll stress his good schooling but add that he needs plenty of work. We can put "genuine reason for sale" – well, there is, isn't there?'

'Yes,' I said, 'he's schizophrenic!'

That night I scarcely slept. Patchy's strong point was his remarkable empathy with the nervous and uncertain, a sympathetic understanding that was difficult to describe. And yet . . . Supposing in a fit of frustration he used his new-found technique on an unsuspecting, trusting, insecure child?

By dawn my mind was made up. I could not live with myself if such a possibility hung over my head, and I had been responsible for the sale.

'But what are the alternatives?' asked George glumly, absent-mindedly buttering both sides of the same piece of toast. 'A dealer? The knacker? A lifetime of broken shins and fences? The third is definitely OUT.'

So was the second. Patchy was only seven years old, and I could not blot from my mind the hours of chuckling happiness he had given to so many desperate little souls.

So that was it: a dealer it would have to be.

'They are, after all, professionals,' I said trying to convince myself as much as George.

'We'll explain the situation and simply ask for a fair price. They're dealing with customers all the time. *They'll* know the best sort of home for him. A one-horse family with plenty of time for him, kind but firm.'

We looked up Yellow Pages and selected a name at random and within reasonable distance.

'Yes, madam,' said a pleasant female voice. 'When would you like us to come? We could manage later today. We'll be in that direction at about 3.30 p.m.'

'That will do nicely,' I said. 'Rosemary!' I yelled out of the kitchen window, 'Get Patchy in and give him a good grooming. We're going to have visitors.'

Rosemary looked decidedly apprehensive but went off, her pert pigtails, which belied her twenty-three years ('so much easier to keep clean') sticking out defiantly. No schizo pony would get the better of her!

An enormous horse-box arrived at exactly 3.30 p.m., seemingly big enough to house an entire cavalry.

An incredibly long, thin man stepped out with a thin nose in a thin face under thinning grey hair.

'Afternoon,' he said in a thin voice. He was followed by a curvaceous young woman in tight jeans, with a mop of unruly dark hair entangled round hooped gold ear-rings. Behind the heavily applied mascara, the hazel eyes were unblinking and hard.

'Where's the pony then?' she said. Clearly the finer points of polite social exchange were not for her.

As if on cue Rosemary appeared round the house leading Patchy.

'Mm-mm,' said the thin man, 'There isn't much call for skewbalds.'

'Would you like Rosemary to ride him for you?' George asked.

'No, thanks. I'll do it,' said the young woman. 'Hat!' she shouted up to the driver's cab of the horse-box, and a child's arm appeared dangling an ancient hard hat by the chin strap. She rammed it on her unruly head, took the reins from Rosemary, and without another word, led Patchy into the manège.

Patchy's performance was impeccable, but then, so was his rider's. There is a saying that a good rider seems to be part of the horse. This one certainly was. Patchy's transitions were smoothly faultless, his paces even and steady, without a hint of his former lameness. The second time round his rider pulled off her hat, confident of her safety, and tossed it over the fence on the grass. Then she cantered him, round and round, hair flowing and ear-rings swinging with curious gaiety that evoked childish memories. I could see in my mind's eye the gleam of spangled tights, the toss of plumes and hear the stirring strains of a circus band. I almost expected her to rise and balance on ballet points on the smoothly flowing back.

Patchy was clearly enjoying it too. Suddenly she turned him towards a low, coloured jump. Surprised but game, he cleared it with inches to spare. No-one had asked him to jump for a very long time.

The next time round, she tried another, higher and wider. Together they sailed over it, black hair and black tail flying in harmony.

'Wind's goin',' said a thin voice beside me.

'What?' said George, as spellbound as I was.

'I said 'is wind's goin'. Listen.'

We listened.

At each third beat of the canter Patchy was giving a low but distinct grunt.

'But that's ridiculous,' I said. 'He's only seven, and he hasn't done enough work to affect his wind. He's never coughed in his life.'

'You can 'ear for yerself,' he said unmoved. 'Might be all right for a bit of 'ackin' or a companion. Not much else.'

Speechless, I gazed at the two as they whirled round the schooling area yet again. Some instinct made me glance towards the house where the long french windows looked directly on to the manège. Each time they passed they were reflected in the glass. And then I saw it. Or did I? The offside toe, the one out of our immediate sight, was twisted in a most unusual way under Patchy's midriff, and with each triple beat of the canter was pressed inwards with a sharp jab, and Patchy grunted.

'George,' I whispered, 'go round to the other side.'

Some urgency in my tone or expression made George obey without question. As I expected, the moment he got there, the thin voice rasped out,

'OK, Tina, I've seen enough.'

Tina slid off Patchy's back with the liquid grace of a cat and led him back to the drive where he eyed the rose bushes speculatively.

'Might be able to place 'im,' said Mr Thin. 'Pity 'e's a skew-bald and 'is wind goin', but you never know. There's always somebody lookin' for nothin' in particular. 'Ow much?' and he produced a roll of notes.

'Four-fifty,' said George, that being the figure we had decided would give a dealer a fair margin of profit for a well-schooled pony.

Mr Thin gave an excellent impression of amused surprise.

'*That* colour?' he said, 'Sorry, three-fifty's me limit and that's generous. With that wind trouble I'll be lucky to get 'im off me 'ands.'

'But there's nothing wrong with his wind,' I protested, still non-plussed by the blatant trickery.

'You 'eard it,' he said unmoved. 'OK,' he added confidentially to George, 'I'll make it three-sixty as the lady 'ere seems to 'ave problems.'

'Four-twenty-five then,' said George, stony-faced.

Mr Thin gave a whimsical shrug and began to place the roll of notes back in his pocket with slow deliberation.

I watched them disappearing and thought of George's endless parade of broken fences, kicked shins, and Patchy's bloated, riderless future.

'Damn you,' I thought, suddenly angry and tired, 'I'll beat you at your own game.'

I swivelled on my stick. 'Rosemary dear,' I called in honey-sweet tones. 'You can take Patchy back now. We've finished with him.'

The effect was electrifying. The hand with the notes stopped, motionless, as if frozen in time. Tina spun round and looked her companion straight in the face, the hard hazel eyes transmitting a message as if in letters ten feet high. Patchy took a step towards the roses.

Mr Thin's Adam's apple leapt convulsively up his scraggy throat.

'Er – come to think of it,' he said, 'I might know just the very person that'd be interested. Always 'ad a bit of a thing about skewbalds, 'e 'as. OK, I'll meet you 'alf way. Four 'undred. Now which of you wants the cash?' he asked George. 'You or the missis?'

'My wife will take it,' said George. 'It's her pony.' We exchanged a brief glance. Four hundred was the figure we had agreed to be talked down to.

The dealer meticulously sorted out his roll of notes. I leaned on my stick with one hand and held out the other.

'I've got six fifties,' he said. 'The rest'll 'ave to be in fivers.'

He counted six fifty-pound notes into my hand and I promptly passed them over to George. He took a long time with the fivers, which were entangled, it seemed, in a rubber band.

'That'll be twenty fivers all told,' he said and started to count them, one by one.

'One, two, three, four, five, six . . . What 'appened to you then?'

I explained briefly the circumstances of my accident.

'Well, I never. As simple as that? Eight, nine, ten, eleven twelve. Nice little pony, that. Got any more you want taken off yer 'ands? Fourteen, fifteen, sixteen.'

George said yes we had and indicated Rashir grazing quietly in the front paddock.

Mr Thin looked up and shook his head. ' 'Aven't got the customers for that sort of quality,' he said. 'Ponies mostly with us. Eighteen, nineteen, twenty. There, that's it. Four 'undred in all.'

I was dumfounded. Did my physical disability make me look like some sort of idiot as well? The trick he was pulling was one of the oldest in the book, older than Music Hall itself. A century of comedians had beguiled half-drunk audiences with its humorous audacity.

'Not quite,' cut in George's voice smoothly. 'Three more to come yet.'

'Can't be. Me 'and's empty. Twenty fivers I 'ad and now your wife's got 'em. You saw me count them in 'er 'and.'

George gave an ominously controlled sigh.

'Count them back into mine then,' he said. There were seventeen.

'Well, I'm blowed,' the thin voice had an apologetic whine. ' 'Ow ever did I manage that? 'Alf a mo, I've got some change in me back pocket,' and he produced exactly three fivers from his rear.

By now Rosemary had unobtrusively joined the scene and exchanged Patchy's tack for a headcollar and lead rein. Tina, obviously anxious to get her bargain away as quickly as possible was leading a solemn Patchy towards the horse-box.

Despite it all, my conscience still niggled. I simply had to say my piece.

'He's a good little chap,' I called out. 'But do warn his new owners that he *can* be a bit of a handful in the paddock, if he gets his own way. Nothing vicious, of course,' I added lamely.

She smiled for the first time, and it was amazing how the brief flash of white teeth transformed the gipsy face.

'Work'll fix that,' she said.

I tried again. 'Keep an eye on him when there's food about . . .'

But it fell on deaf ears; she continued on her way. The deal was obviously concluded and any observations of ours were of no importance whatsoever.

'Forget it,' said George, his hand on my arm, 'you can't do any more.'

Mr Thin had disappeared into the driver's cab. George, Rosemary and I stood silently waiting for the moment of truth.

To reach the parked horse-box Tina and Patchy had to pass a stretch of grass known affectionately as The Waste Land. Too small for a paddock, too big for a lawn and too bumpy for a car park it was left to grow lusciously wild.

At the time of Patchy's departure the young spring grass was at its juicy best. A brief shower only an hour before had spangled the bright emerald green with a gentle shimmer of diamond drops. Bees were busily investigating the first bright buttercups and a faint perfume of early, sun-warmed clover hung in the air.

Fascinated, the three of us watched as Tina led her charge along its edge, the lead rein resting loosely in her left hand. Twice the pony's ears twitched forwards and sideways, his tail giving an anticipatory swish. Any minute now, I thought. But a slim hand resting lightly on his withers moved unerringly up his neck and gripped firmly at the poll. They both walked straight into the box.

We watched the huge vehicle manoeuvre its way out of the drive and away.

'I'll be damned!' said George, in a neat reversal of my own earlier thoughts.

'She's very experienced,' I said, 'She must . . .'

'I don't mean *that*,' exploded George, 'But while we've been gawping here they've loaded that pony with *our* headcollar and leading rein. And you know what they cost!'

I did. The headcollar was a good quality leather one. Between them, the two items must have been worth about fifteen pounds.

The next day was Sunday and I was looking forward to a restful, lazy morning, conscience free. We had done our best, and now it was someone else's responsibility.

I felt a pang of sadness. What could the future of such a little mixed-up character be – so full of loving co-operation one minute, so unpredictably dangerous the next? Had I done enough for him? I had heard of personality changes in people after a traumatic experience. Could it really happen to a pony, or had a sequence of events merely uncovered a latent streak? Was there anything else we could have . . .?

'I've brought you a cup of tea,' said George. 'I thought we'd pop over and see how Patchy's settled in. I feel quite sentimental about the crazy little chap.'

'But won't they be a bit surprised?' I asked, trying to snuggle back under the duvet.

'I don't think so. Anyway, I want to see their set-up. We'll say we are considering them for future deals. That'll get them.'

It was nearly lunch time when we finally found their premises, and had to admit grudgingly to each other that we were pleasantly surprised.

Several large buildings were grouped round a well-kept circular drive and there was an atmosphere of cheerful activity. Neither the thin-faced dealer nor Tina were to be seen, but several neatly dressed girl grooms were busily filling buckets and wheeling barrows. The only jarring note was the inevitable tinny sound of an invisible transistor set.

We enquired about Patchy's whereabouts and were directed without hesitation to 'the shed over there'.

'The shed' was the understatement of all time. A vast concrete building, it housed about thirty horses and ponies of every possible size and colour. Each occupied its own airy pen separated from its neighbours by only a low but sturdy double bar.

It was quite a while before we recognised Patchy. Clipped out, shaggy mane neatly hogged, hairy feet trimmed, he looked twice the pony we had sold them, and twice the price.

'Excuse me,' said George to a groom hurrying by with an armful of horse blankets. 'That pony there, he's still got our headcollar and lead rein. Could we have them back please?' Now I knew the real reason for the 'sentimental' visit.

'Are you sure?' she asked. 'We normally use our own.'

'Absolutely,' said George. 'If you look at that disc, you'll see it says 'Apache' and our telephone number.' (The latter had been an inspiration when Patchy took to his wandering ways.)

The girl slipped through the sliding door and inspected the disc.

'You're right,' she said cheerfully. 'Hang on, and I'll get another.'

George could hardly hide his smug satisfaction as he tucked the head collar and lead rein under his arm.

We turned to take a last look at Patchy. On each side of him a quiet pony, one a pretty chesnut, the other a grey, was contentedly picking at a well-filled haynet. Patchy's was empty already, and he was eyeing the low partitions with a calculating expression we had learnt to recognise.

We left as unobtrusively as we came, confident that before long, Patchy, the lovable but unpredictable, would be showing the crafty pair that he too had a trick or two up his stifle.

6 · Pitch and Toss

It had been one of those days when nothing could go wrong. We went from strength to strength, Sable Monarch and I, and it seemed that the big Hanoverian was possessed of a mystic power as he soared like some mythical creature over every jump without a single fault. And now the final glory. What better end to a perfect day than to be seated on a horse with such a name and receive the cup from none other than Her Majesty? I leaned forward, the cheers of the crowd ringing in my ears . . . Hurrah-hurrah . . . rah-rah . . . rah-rah . . . brr-brr . . . brr-brr . . .

I sat bolt upright, my frail moment of triumph shattered, and stared blearily at the clock. Who on earth could be ringing at 6.40 a.m.? There was no sound from the spare room where George had slept since my accident, not from any rift in our relationship, but the sheer need to have ample space to accommodate my restless, aching limb. It was no use. I would have to drag myself away from the warmth and lean over awkwardly to answer the wretched thing.

'Hello?' I said irritably.

'I'm sorry to bother you so early,' said a woman's voice, 'but are you the lady who attends physiotherapy with a broken femur?'

'Yes,' I said tersely. 'Is there something wrong? Have I missed an appointment?' I looked at the clock again; perhaps it had stopped.

'Oh no,' she said brightly, 'but I heard about you in the Nurses Home. I believe you sell horses.'

There were several seconds silence. Now at least the early hour was explained. I knew from experience that 6.40 a.m. was practically the middle of the day in hospital routine.

'Hello, Hello! Are you still there?'

'Yes,' I said sourly, 'but no, I do *not* sell horses, as you put it.'

'Oh, I'm so sorry. I was told that you wouldn't be able to ride again, so you are selling off your horses.'

There was another silence. This was a thought that was never permitted to enter my head.

'I won't be able to ride *for the time being*,' I corrected her bleakly. 'So yes, I am selling off some of our horses, but only to selected people.' Perhaps it was the early hour, but my explanation seemed to have a hollow, hopeless ring.

'I'm so sorry,' she apologised again, and the voice was warmly sympathetic. 'I didn't mean to upset you, but I'm on the staff here, and you know what it's like, rushed off our feet. I like to relax with a bit of riding when I can, Western style, and it would be nice to have my own horse. I've been offered good stabling, cheap, near the hospital. Have you anything reasonable that might do?'

'Do I know you?' I asked. 'Are you in Orthopaedic?'

'Good heavens, no. Maternity!' and she gave a little gurgling chuckle. I could almost smell the baby powder. 'We've had two boys and a girl in the night.'

'Are you an experienced rider?'

'Oh yes, I'm from a farming background really. We farm in Dorset.'

'I might be able to help,' I said, suddenly wide awake. 'When could you get here?'

'We're short-staffed, so I'm doing double duty today, but I could be with you by about four o'clock if I skip tea.'

I remembered the kind hands that had supplied so many cups of tea in my own desperate days of hospital.

'You come straight over,' I said, 'I'll give you some tea.'

In the paddock, Rosemary and I considered the situation. None of our horses had done Western riding as such, but we were confident that, given the right guidance, they would soon respond.

'Did she give any indication of height or weight?' asked Rosemary.

I had to admit that I had not thought to ask about either.

'I think Pitch and Toss would be the best bets,' mused Rosemary. 'Either one or the other will do, depending on her size.'

Pitch and Toss were full brother and sister with only a year between them. By a thoroughbred sire out of a Highland pony mare, they were exactly alike in colour – a beautiful golden dun with dark mane and tail and a dorsal stripe. But there the similarity ended. Pitch, the gelding, had inherited his dam's sturdy frame and feathery feet, while Toss, the mare was a carbon copy of the thoroughbred sire's elegant slimness.

They had acquired their paired nicknames by a strange coincidence. Pitch from his habit, endearing or exasperating according to the mood one was in, of pitching his feed bowl out over the stable door the moment it was empty; and Toss, because of her coquettish habit of tossing her pretty head when flirting in the paddock (and sometimes, alas, with a rider on her back as well).

It was Toss we had actually gone to see when we visited the farmer some miles away, having been told of her dainty elegance and natural jump. While Rosemary tried her out in a nearby field, Pitch had kept pace with her up and down the fence, an expression of anxiety and panic in his dark eyes.

‘ ’E’ll miss ’er, the young ’un,’ said the farmer. ‘Never been apart all their lives.’

We watched the young gelding copying his sister’s every move. When she trotted, he trotted; when she cantered, he cantered; when she stopped, he stopped, and whinnied anxiously.

‘*He* wouldn’t take much schooling,’ commented George. ‘All you’d have to do is show him his sister.’

‘It’s very bad to let two horses become inseparable,’ I said, having read it somewhere in a book. ‘They’ll be difficult to handle apart.’

Nevertheless, as George pointed out, it was silly to waste space in the horse-box, and we bought them both.

‘Yes,’ I agreed with Rosemary, ‘Pitch or Toss might do nicely. You often see golden duns in Western films, so one or the other might be just what she’s looking for.’

A rather ancient Beetle reached our front door just after four and Penny Williams stepped out. She was just as I had imagined her, with plump rosy cheeks, kind grey eyes and an engaging dimple. Wispy hair sprang out in all directions from an untidy bun, and there was a waft of disinfectant as she peeled off her jacket to reveal a full figure under a sweater and jeans. She had exactly the sort of comforting presence that an expectant mum would want beside her at her Finest Hour.

‘I’m sorry I’m so scruffy,’ she said, ‘I’ve had such a rush getting changed. We’ve just had another baby girl. I *told* them it would be a girl, but they wouldn’t believe me. Oh-h, is that the teapot? I’m dying of thirst.’

Over her second cup of tea and third slice of cake she began to relax.

‘I really shouldn’t,’ she grinned, tapping her waistline ruefully, ‘but it’s such a change from the hospital dishwater and cardboard.’

She delved into a copious handbag and produced a sheaf of photographs.

'Let me show you these,' she spluttered eagerly through a mouthful of crumbs. 'These were our horses before I took up hospital work.'

They were a motley collection of fairly well-groomed animals. Penny with two hairy skewbald ponies; her teenage brother leading a skittish Welsh cob; a beautiful bay hunter with Penny, hatless, in the saddle; Penny and her sister (unexpectedly blonde) stroking the nose of a fine dapple grey.

'Only the skewbalds are left,' she explained wistfully. 'My sister's working in London, and my brother rides but doesn't know enough stable management to be responsible. We sold the hunter to a Canadian who took it back with him, and we got quite a good sum for him.'

I knew how she felt.

'Never mind. With a bit of luck maybe you'll soon be riding again, especially if you've got good stabling close to the hospital.'

She brightened visibly. 'Do let's go and look at yours. I can't wait!'

Out in the yard she crooned with delight over Pitch and Toss. 'Aren't they both *beautiful*,' she breathed. 'I don't know which I like best. And that colour! Just right for Western gear!'

'Which would you like to try? Although you're a bit on the bonny side,' she giggled at my choice of word, 'you're not very tall, so either would do. But, of course, the gelding is younger and still very green. The mare's a lovely ride but a bit full of herself. Take your pick.'

'Oo-oo! the mare, please. She's lovely.'

'What about a hard hat and boots?' Rosemary's voice cut in, a shade tartly.

Penny's face reddened.

'Nurse Williams has come straight from the hospital,' I said curtly. 'She may borrow my hat – and boots, too, if they fit.'

Rosemary tacked up Toss in silence and led her to the

manège. Penny, in my hard hat and boots, a size too big, clambered laboriously into the saddle.

'Gosh!' she grunted, 'I'm out of practice.'

Her riding was adequate but no more. But then, I reflected, with her irregular hours, what more could one expect? Toss lived up to her name and showed a certain contempt for the out-of-practice hands, but responded obediently enough. She took two jumps smoothly despite Penny's clumsy mishandling of the reins and heavy landings.

Rosemary looked on with marked disapproval.

'I'm not giving a very good account of myself, am I?' gasped Penny as she came to a halt, perspiring noticeably. 'Actually, I'm more used to a Western saddle. I'm quite good then.'

Dismounted, she stroked Toss's golden neck thoughtfully.

'I like her very much, and I really *do* ride better, Western style. How much do you want for her?'

I looked carefully to see if Rosemary was out of earshot then named the figure, knocking a hundred off in view of her hard-pressed profession.

'That's *wonderful*,' she beamed, 'I can afford that. I might even manage a new saddle as well. My old one's a bit battered and she deserves the best. If I can get one fairly quickly, a Western one, I mean, can I try her with it before I finally decide, just to make sure she likes it?'

'Of course.' It was, after all, a sensible request. 'When would you like to come back?'

'As soon as I can find the right saddle. I don't suppose you know somewhere fairly near where I might get a good one? I get so little time off at the hospital to hunt around.'

Suddenly I remembered the rather self-conscious, gleaming display of Western gear I had seen in the side window of our local saddlers. An old, established family firm, they had made the gesture grudgingly – 'traditional hunting requirements' were more in their line. But as old Mr Gregory, the white-haired owner said, 'One has to move with the times, and there's no accounting for changing tastes, especially in the young.' I jotted down the address on an old envelope and gave it to Penny.

'Great!' More strands of hair sprouted out of her bun in her enthusiasm. 'I'll pop round tomorrow when I come off duty, then ring you later.'

The following evening a rather tired Penny rang. She had managed to get a saddle by skipping lunch, could she come round early next day? She could fix it by switching duties.

'Come about eleven,' I suggested. 'Then you can have coffee with us before you start.'

'You're *such* a kind person,' she sounded half asleep. 'I'll be there.'

'This I must see,' said George, when I told him of the arrangements. 'I've always wondered about the difference between Western riding and the usual sort. Now I can see at first hand.'

When Penny arrived the next morning we were momentarily taken aback. Sporting a checked open-necked shirt, flapping leather chaps and fancy boots, she wore an enormous Stetson rammed on to a curtain of flowing, untidy hair. In her arms, almost hiding her face, she carried the most elaborate saddle I had ever seen, resplendent in tooled black leather and metal studs.

'I got it on a discount,' she puffed with a grin, hitching the weight further up her arms. 'I just can't wait to try it out.' Coffee was forgotten by all of us.

Toss's first reaction to all this splendour was a distinctly nervous one, but Penny produced a bright, Mexican style blanket, folded it in four and gently placed it on her back.

'To protect her spine,' she whispered confidentially. 'She won't be used to the different spread of weight.'

Once in position, we had to admit, the elaborate saddle and bridle looked truly impressive, set off to perfection by Toss's golden coat, and flowing mane and tail.

'The schooling area's a bit cramped,' said our new cowgirl. 'Is there somewhere more open we could try?'

'Certainly,' George seemed bewitched by the whole extraordinary scene. 'We'll all go through to the paddocks, there's plenty of space there.'

As Penny was led away through the spinney by a rather cool Rosemary, she called back to George, 'My camera's in the car. It might be fun to take some pictures.'

George went back for it with alacrity. Clearly he agreed.

Toss behaved extremely well despite the oddity of her unfamiliar trappings, trotting, cantering and turning with only the occasional toss of disapproval. Penny's riding remained unimpressive, but she seemed more relaxed in the Western seat.

It was not long before we were joined by another spectator. Pitch, at the far end of the next paddock, came cantering over to see what on earth his sister was up to, and immediately began his 'mirror' performance on the other side of the fence, mimicking the pair's every action almost to perfection.

'I've never seen anything like it!' Penny gasped in astonishment. 'Do you suppose he would do it, side by side, on a lead rein? It would be just like a rodeo stunt!'

'Rodeo stunt!' muttered Rosemary as she went to fetch a headcollar.

The experiment was not entirely a success. Reins and stirrups became hopelessly entangled as the young gelding did his best to join in the fun. Through it all, Penny laughed and chuckled unafraid, until at last she was able to canter them both, side by side, the full length of the field, steadily gaining speed as they went. We could almost see the rails of the old corral in the background and John Wayne leaning on the nearest post.

'Do take some pictures!' she called, and gave George some rapid fire instructions as to the workings of her camera as she hurtled past.

'I think,' said Rosemary, twirling a pigtail with nervous fingers, 'they ought to stop soon. Pitch is beginning to hot up. He's too young to be doing this sort of thing, and there could be an accident.'

'Just a few more shots!' George was obviously carried away by the excitement.

'Stop!' called out Rosemary a few seconds later and stepped out authoritatively into their path just as the uncontrolled canter was in danger of becoming a galloping stampede.

Toss knew that voice well. She had, in fact, always been particularly responsive to the vocal command, and she pulled up smartly on her haunches in true wild west fashion, while Pitch managed something close to a dramatic air-pawing half-rear.

'Yaa-hoo!' yelled Penny. 'That sure was GREAT!'

'I'll hold them while you dismount,' said Rosemary coldly, and led the two excited horses away with quiet skill.

Walking back to the house, thumbs stuck in her belt, Penny became suddenly solemn.

'I'm going to ask you a funny sort of question,' she said at length. 'I hope you won't be too surprised.'

'Go ahead.' George was immediately wary.

'Would you consider, well, would you be agreeable to . . .'

Here comes the hard-luck story, cashwise, I thought. Underpaid nurses, and all that, and exchanged a glance with George who was putting the camera in its case with elaborate care.

'I mean, would you think me crazy if I asked to buy *both*? There's room at the stables.'

George almost dropped the camera, and I stupidly tripped over my own stick.

'You see, my brother's nearly eighteen, and we could ride together when I get back to the farm. And I *did* make quite a bit on the hunter. But if you could manage just a *little* price adjustment on the two it would help.'

Twenty minutes later over the belated coffee they came to an amicable agreement, subject to Penny's solemn promise that both animals would continue to have some serious schooling, the young gelding in particular.

'It'll take a couple of days for the banker's draft to come

through.' Penny munched happily on her fourth Abernethy biscuit. 'So shall we say between eleven and twelve on Friday? and, please don't be offended, but I'll bring my vet, just as a formality you understand. It's a rule I promised my father not to break. I expect you know our vet,' and she gave a name that left us speechless, an exalted personage who attended the equine favourites of royalty, no less.

Clambering into her Beetle she threw the enormous Stetson into the back, then arranged the elaborate saddle and all its trappings with loving care on the passenger seat beside her.

'I'm *so* happy,' she dimpled up at us, 'I can't remember when I've been so happy. It makes up for all the hard grind at the hospital. Did you manage to get some good pictures?'

'Yes, some first class shots!' George was still in a pink daze at our unexpected good luck.

'Great!' she called back as she put the car into gear. 'I'll sort out the best and give you a copy. Gosh! I'd better get going, we're expecting twins some time today.'

On the Friday, Rosemary arrived at the yard a good hour early.

'Everything's got to be perfect,' she explained. 'With *that* man coming we can't afford to cut corners – and it's not as if I get much help,' she added darkly.

We were now down to a single working pupil. Linda had departed to another establishment, having given the required notice, on the grounds that, as we no longer had any students, she could get no teaching practice, a fair enough observation.

The one remaining girl rejoiced under the name of Marigold, despite listless mousey hair, a long, sallow face and an even sallower disposition. She had the gift of making the simplest task appear to be a lifetime's burden.

By the time she arrived, ten minutes late, Rosemary had mucked out the boxes, banished the dirty straw, and brought the astonished Pitch and Toss in from their favourite paddock.

'Clean straw for all the boxes,' she ordered, 'then scrub out the feed bowls and water buckets.'

'But I did them the day before yesterday,' wailed Marigold.

'Then do them again. And when you've done that, check all the grooming kit, and make sure the headcollars have got *matching* lead reins.'

'Who the heck's coming, royalty?'

'As good as. So get moving.'

'But what about the yard?' Marigold had discovered that sweeping the yard required little mental effort and could be comfortably stretched out to look like a sweating, onerous drudge.

'Do it when you've finished the other things, then go over it again at 10.15 exactly. In between, I want you to help with grooming and shampooing.'

'Shampooing!'

'You heard.'

Rosemary was already smothering Toss with a copious lathering of Sunsilk shampoo, while Pitch watched apprehensively from Box 3, obviously uncomfortably aware that he might be next. A large bottle of Fairy Liquid and a bowl of fresh water stood nearby.

'For manes and tails,' explained Rosemary. 'It makes the hairs glisten, like spun glass.'

'Wh-what can I do to help?' I offered, miserably aware of my own inadequacy and cumbersome stick.

'There's the cloakroom. He may want to wash his hands. We could do with some more paper towels and a new bar of soap.'

I teetered back to the house and returned with bleach, Ajax (non-scratch), a packet of fresh towels for the container and a new bar of Lifebuoy soap. After cleaning the wash-basin, I ran the tap over the soap so that it would not look too obviously new, then placed it carefully in position. I also gave the window a quick rub over and replaced the air-freshener in the toilet with a somewhat sickly 'Spring Bouquet'. Looking down, it was apparent that Marigold's yard-sweeping tactics had a distinct line of demarcation. Wisps of straw and blobs of mud adhered to the concrete floor. I searched for a brush, and swept it vigorously.

'Watch it!' my right hip warned me sharply, giving a sudden, stabbing pain as a cue.

At 10.25 a perspiring but triumphant Rosemary called me out to inspect the yard. Marigold was just finishing the last strokes of her second sweeping, wearing her best, overworked, hard-done-by expression. I felt a glow of pride, and was momentarily transported back to my first encounter with The Squire and his impressive surroundings. Ours were every bit as good. All was immaculate, down to the last coiled lead rein with its matching headcollar at each door.

Pitch and Toss occupied Boxes 2 and 3, and Rosemary had chosen their immediate neighbours with great care. In Box 1 our prize possession, Angelo, an exquisite Cremello, surveyed the scene with tranquil aquamarine eyes, guaranteed to stop the most blasé visitor in his tracks. In Box 4, the solemn Webster dozed quietly over the door, glad of the opportunity to do absolutely nothing officially.

'Congratulations!' I said warmly. 'Everything looks simply beautiful. But you're very early; they won't be here until at least eleven o'clock.'

'Ah,' Rosemary gave me a direct look. 'I know these types. They make a point of arriving early to see what you might be covering up. But they won't catch *me* on the hop,' then, glancing at her hoof-oil rimmed nails, 'but look at me! I must tidy myself up, and *you*, Marigold!' Marigold almost dropped her brush at the urgency of her tone. 'Get into your clean jods and tidy your hair, but don't mess up the wash-basin, it's just been cleaned.'

'Come into the house, Rosemary,' I said soothingly, 'and freshen up there. I'll keep watch from the kitchen window.'

Ten minutes later I heard the sound of a car in the drive.

'Rosemary!' I whispered hoarsely through the cloakroom door, 'I think they're here!'

'I *knew* it,' came an agonised wail from the other side. 'Oh, this damn zip, it won't pull up!'

'Take your time. I'll forestall them with a few pleasantries.'

I selected my best stick, the one with the carved horse's head (I had quite a collection) glanced at the hall mirror and opened the door, to step out with what I hoped would be relaxed but business-like charm. It was the postman.

'Sorry, madam,' he said, 'I couldn't get it in the letter box,' and handed me George's long-awaited seed catalogue.

When Rosemary did emerge, the transformation was remarkable. Immaculate black boots were topped by equally immaculate beige jodhpurs, and a crisp, pale blue shirt revealed a neat little waist and shapely bosom. A darker blue tie was held in place by a silver pin, and her usually errant pigtails were tamed into tidy, twin coils in the nape of her neck. A discreet brush of mascara and a touch of fresh lipstick, and the picture of well-dressed efficiency was complete.

'Rosemary!' I exclaimed, genuinely delighted, 'you look marvellous!' and it suddenly struck me how little I really knew about this girl on whom I depended so much. Hardworking and reliable, conscientious to a fault over her equine charges, she was always there, sensibly clad. Why had I never noticed how pretty she was? What did she do at the end of her busy day? Did she change into a dress or skirt? In all the time I had known her I had never seen her legs, as pretty no doubt, as the rest of her.

Then I remembered her quiet support on that fateful day, and a lump came in my throat.

'Let the whole world come to inspect us, Rosemary,' I said, 'I shall be proud of you, your yard and your horses.'

'Thank you.' She was stuffing her soiled jeans into a plastic bag to hide her embarrassment. A faint whiff of Eau de Cologne accompanied the action; it made a pleasant change from the more usual Eau de Cheval.

'What exactly do you want me to do?' She was practical as ever.

'Just potter about in the yard, nothing strenuous, and I'll do some dead-heading to the roses in the front. When I see the car turn into the far end of the lane, I'll give you the signal, then just stand by Toss's box.'

At eleven o'clock an expectant hush descended on the place. Hardly a sound came from the yard where Rosemary and Marigold were talking in lowered tones, and the horses chomped peacefully at their ration of hay. The two stable cats sat like silent sentinels on the rockery and the dog dozed off in the porch. Only the sharp click-clicking of my clippers interrupted the drowsy humming of a bee.

I began to feel ridiculously like one of those insipid, chiffon-clad females in drawing-room comedies who were for ever appearing at french windows from a painted back-drop garden, carrying a trug of fresh-cut flowers – except that mine were wizened and dead.

A totally blank half-hour had passed when Marigold appeared round the corner of the house, self-conscious in her clean jodhpurs.

'Rosemary says will it be all right if we have a quick cup of coffee and biscuits? We're both famished after all that *extra* work.' She managed to sound as if she, at least, was at death's door with starvation.

I managed an over-bright smile. 'Of course, that's the best way to make them arrive! The moment you take your first sip, they'll be here. It never fails!'

Had they been delayed? Penny did say *between* eleven and twelve. If they were not coming, surely they would have rung by now?

By mid-day there wasn't a single dead-head left on the roses, and I was just contemplating a half-hearted attack on the clematis when the phone rang shrilly through the front door, startling the slumbering dog out of its wits.

I hobbled in quickly minus my stick.

'Watch it, I said,' warned my hip again, with another sharp stab of pain.

'Five-one-three-four?' I elocuted into the receiver in carefully modulated tones, then, rather ungraciously, 'Oh, it's you,' as

George's voice answered.

George picked up my tension immediately.

'Haven't they turned up yet?'

'No, we've been ready for over an hour.'

'I expect they've been delayed, an emergency probably, a road accident or something. You can never be sure with a vet and he's coming quite a distance. I'll ring off in case they're trying to get through.'

I went back to the clematis.

Some time later a persistent rap-rap-rapping began in the yard.

'It's Pitch,' explained Rosemary looking decidedly worried when I went to investigate. 'He doesn't like being shut up too long, and he's discovered the noise he can make if he bangs the door. Toss isn't much better either. She's walking round and round her box like a caged tiger. I can't let them get away with it; it can develop into a habit. What shall I do? They're very late, aren't they? Haven't they phoned?'

True to their dam's ancestry, Pitch and Toss, both of them still youngsters, much preferred the wide open spaces, only tolerating the restrictions of a box for as long as they considered necessary.

I looked up at the indeterminate grey sky.

'Let them out into the yard paddock for a while. They can get rid of their energy, and I don't think it'll rain.'

The yard paddock was a modest quarter-acre close to the boxes where we occasionally put the horses for convenience while dealing with general stable-management.

'It had better not, after all the work I've put in on them.' Rosemary managed to look both apprehensive and relieved that the decision had been taken from her.

I was soon to regret it. The paddock gate was hardly closed behind the two animals when the first slow ominous drops began to fall, increasing steadily in number and size. Pitch, delighted with his new freedom, began to dig enthusiastically at the dampening ground to make sure of a suitably muddy patch, then stepped back obligingly to let his beloved sister have the first glorious, sticky roll.

One look at Rosemary's stricken face and my patience gave way.

'I'm going to phone,' I glowered. 'This is not good enough. It's nearly lunch-time, and I don't care how important he is, the least they could do is ring!'

I knew the hospital number only too well.

'Maternity, please,' I said to the switchboard girl.

'Ward Three, Maternity.'

'I'm sorry to trouble you, but I should like to speak to Penny Williams rather urgently – is that possible?'

'I'm sorry she's not here at the moment. She might be at Extension twenty-one.'

That at least was reassuring. I felt a vague relief that the name was obviously familiar, and that she genuinely was not on duty.

'I'll put you through,' continued the helpful voice.

'Extension twenty-one.'

'May I speak to Penny Williams, please?'

'I'm sorry she's not here. Can I give her a message?'

'Not really, I've been expecting her here. She's probably on her way over.'

'Oh, are you the lady with the horses?'

'Yes?' I said hopefully.

'There's a message here on the pad for you. It says she's sorry she's had to change duty in an emergency, and can't get over today, but she'll be in touch.'

'Does she say anything about the vet?'

'The bet?'

'No, the VET – V-E-T.'

'N-no, the only other message here is for the laundry.'

'I see. Thank you.'

I put the receiver down feeling numb and deflated, and looked out of the kitchen window at the two drenched figures leading muddy and bedraggled horses back to the stables.

'It's all off, girls,' I called flatly. 'Take it easy for the rest of the day, and Rosemary, arrange things so that you can leave an hour early.'

Rosemary looked straight towards me, an inscrutable expression in her eyes that I had never seen before.

When four whole days had passed and the phone remained obstinately silent, it was George's anger that finally boiled over as we watched the two animals being led in and led out, groomed and re-groomed 'just in case'.

'Get on the phone to the Ward Sister, or even the *Matron*, if necessary,' he growled. 'That might shake Miss Williams into some sort of explanation.'

For the second time I spoke to the hospital switchboard girl and asked for the appropriate extension.

'Ward Three, Maternity. Sister speaking.' I was a little nonplussed that Sister herself had picked up the telephone.

'I'm so sorry to trouble you,' I said nervously, 'I know how busy you must be, but I'm trying to contact Nurse Williams. Is she available?'

'Nurse Williams? There's no-one by that name on the staff here.'

I felt a tightening at my throat. 'But she said she worked in the Maternity ward.'

'Just a moment, please.'

There was a click as she put the receiver down, then a silence. I felt a growing queasiness in the pit of my stomach.

'Hello! There *was* a Penny Williams here,' said the matter-of-fact voice, 'but she was only a temporary domestic, a student vacation job. She left at the week-end. Is it urgent?'

'N-no,' my voice didn't seem to belong to me, 'she was just enquiring about buying a horse.'

'A horse?'

It was clear that as far as Sister was concerned I might as well have said dinosaur.

'I doubt very much whether she could afford to buy a horse, but I can give you a forwarding address.'

Another silence, then she read out the address carefully. It was a Dorsetshire farm.

'I'm so sorry I can't be of more help,' she said briskly, 'but, of course, I didn't know her personally, and she wasn't here very long.'

That night George sat down grimly and wrote a terse note to be sent by Certificate of Posting. It was returned three days later marked 'Not known at this address'. The flap had quite clearly been steamed open and resealed.

When I broke the news to Rosemary, her reaction was unexpected.

'I thought so,' she said calmly. 'I suspected she might be a time-waster all along, but I thought she was a friend of yours from the hospital. I didn't like her from the start.'

'So I noticed,' I said wearily. 'Oh well, we all have to learn.'

It was some time later that George and I called at the local saddlers to pick up some wormers and hoof-oil.

White-haired Mr Gregory beamed at us benevolently over his mahogany counter.

'I was *so* sorry the Western saddle wasn't suitable,' he said. 'As I explained to the young lady, we don't usually let tack out on approval, but, of course, you are a customer of long standing, and in your case –' he glanced surreptitiously at my stick, 'the right fitting is absolutely essential, after your accident. The young lady, a nurse I understand, explained your difficulties, and we managed to polish out the few scratches quite successfully.'

He bent down and lifted a white plastic bag from under the counter. The smile behind the gold-rimmed glasses had taken on a slightly frosty look.

'You will understand, I'm sure, about the blanket. We can't put it back in stock. It's rather – er – sweat-stained I'm afraid, so I've taken the liberty of adding it to your monthly account. Minus the usual discount, of course.'

Dumbfounded, I attempted an unconcerned smile, and took

the bag from him. A faint smell of horse wafted from its pseudo-Mexican contents as we were bowed out of the shop with Victorian charm.

We drove home in total silence. In the soothing comfort of our own kitchen I was the first to speak.

'So! We've met our first time-waster. I wonder whether they were really her brother and sister in the photographs, or simply the real owners.'

'Worse than that,' said George, '*I* wonder how many people are being conned into giving free rides on the strength of the latest addition to her collection – "Penny with her two golden duns, Western style" – obligingly taken by muggins himself.'

7 · Webster

The girl at Check-out Three was friendly and helpful as ever, a welcome contrast to her bored clock-watching counterparts at Numbers One, Two and Four.

'Don't forget this,' she said cheerily, carefully moving my walking stick from the handle of the now empty trolley to the full one.

She was not to know how great a milestone she had just marked with those few words, for I had indeed forgotten it, and was preparing to leave the store for the car park with my load just like all the other shoppers around me.

The day I made the triumphant if painful discovery that I could drive the car again ('only for short distances, mind,' George had said) I made an equally important one – that I could 'drive' a supermarket trolley as well. Provided that I was careful to avoid one of those demoniac specimens with minds of their own, known to all exasperated supermarket shoppers, I could hook my stick on the handle, lean my full weight on the trolley and zoom around muttering about rising prices with the best of them. I also found out that the least busy times at the store were immediately before or after lunch, and that the girl at Check-out Three, red-haired and green-eyed was a tonic in herself.

Without once referring to my disability directly, she personally wrapped up my frozen goods, and transferred all my groceries from one trolley to another, then pushed it away within easy reach.

Her heart-warming smile, flashing through bright peach-coloured lips was the best discount any store could offer. All I knew about her was that her name was 'Ginge', an obvious reference to her carroty locks, abbreviated to the obligatory monosyllable by her counterparts Deb, Fran and Trish, whose aim it seemed was to make anything to do with work as brief as possible.

On this particular day I was the only customer at that Check-out and Ginge was especially attentive. With no-one in earshot she spoke for the first time of my secret.

'Arthritis is it?' she asked. 'My mum's got arthritis, but she can't get about like you.'

'No,' I felt this was one I had to put straight. 'I parted company from my horse.'

Ginge's eyes widened under their spiky mascara.

'Do you go horse-riding then? How did it happen? Hunting?'

'No – I, well, it's a long story,' I said lamely. Over the months I had found it increasingly tedious and embarrassing to have to explain in detail how I had fallen off a horse that was actually standing still; and by now we had been joined by a ferrety-faced woman with a trolley-load of packaged and tinned foods, and a youngster tugging at her skirt.

But Ginge was not to be put off by the new arrival.

'Was it your own horse?'

'Yes.'

'Have you still got it?'

'Yes.'

The ferrety-faced woman ostentatiously put a tin of sliced peaches and a bag of sugar on the check-out counter.

'I ride too,' went on Ginge leaning on her till confidentially. 'I don't suppose you know anyone who's got a nice pony for sale do you? My husband says he'll buy me one if I'll go and work in his garage. You know – secretary, receptionist, tea-maker, general dogsbody stuff. I've been looking, but it's a bit of a gamble, isn't it, not knowing the people or the horse.'

A five pound bag of potatoes joined the tinned peaches and sugar with an ominous thump. Ferrety-face Junior began investigating a nearby display of Smarties.

'Well, I might be able to help.' I said in astonishment. 'Actually we've got several . . .'

'Did you say "several"? Are you a dealer then?'

'No, definitely not.' The saga of Patchy was still fresh in my mind.

'I didn't think you were. Not the type. But how . . .'

A loud howl interrupted her as Ferrety-face Junior was hauled back from the Smarties and soundly smacked.

'If it's not *too* much trouble,' said his mother acidly, 'I would like to get out of here.'

Embarrassed, I grabbed Ginge's ball-point pen from the till and scribbled on the back of an old check-out slip.

'That's my phone number and address,' I mumbled. 'Contact me if you like. I'm usually in.'

That afternoon, tired from my solo sojourn in the Big Wide World again, I was resting, feet up, as per George's orders, when the low purring of a well-bred car drifted through the open window. I looked out in time to see a sleek, pale-coloured Porsche stop at the front door and a dark-haired young woman in an expensive suede jacket and well-cut trousers get out. She was a total stranger, and I groaned to myself as I slipped on my shoes ready to give the inevitable directions to this or that obscure village address. But she closed the door firmly behind her. Clearly the visit was to be a prolonged one.

As I stepped forward, the mystery was explained; from the other side an orange-bright head appeared like the rising sun over the misty grey horizon of the car roof. I hardly recognised Ginge without her nylon supermarket overall, but the cheery smile seemed even more so above the green polo-necked sweater.

I looked again at the smartly dressed stranger. For some reason, Rosemary's recent words came into my head – 'I know these types, they make a point of arriving early to see what you might be covering up.' Ginge and her companion were going one better, arriving unannounced. I could not in all honesty say 'uninvited'.

'I hope you don't mind,' said Ginge, appearing full length round the car to reveal jodhpurs, riding boots and a hard hat under one arm, 'but this is my half day, and we thought we'd come straight over. This is my best friend,' she added, giving no name.

I shook hands with Best Friend who offered me three cool finger tips in return. I felt distinctly nettled. I had met 'best friends' before; they usually watched with gimlet eyes for every possible fault, either through jealousy, pique or the need to air the supremacy of their knowledge.

Ginge must have noticed my uncertainty.

'Have we come at an awkward time?' She looked genuinely concerned.

'Well, yes, in a way. Rosemary is giving the yard "a good doing" as she calls it, and all the horses are out in the paddocks.'

'That's all right,' said Best Friend levelly. 'It's one way of seeing if there's any trouble with catching.'

I gritted my teeth.

'You, madam,' I thought to myself, 'are in for a surprise.' So for that matter, was I.

Rosemary, with her arms up to the elbows in a bucket of soapy water was not over-enthusiastic either.

'Which one do you want me to fetch?' she asked, reaching for a towel.

'Carry on with what you're doing,' I replied. 'The young lady doesn't know yet which she wants to try. Just give us a headcollar and we'll go through to the paddock ourselves.'

At the paddock gate we leaned over and studied the equine figures dotted across the grass: four geldings to the left of the centre fence and three mares to the right.

'Which are yours?' Ginge was wide-eyed.

'All of them,' I answered casually, and was gratified to see the fleeting flicker of surprise on her friend's face.

I clicked my tongue loudly in the manner universally recognised as encouragement to horses. Seven heads rose simultaneously, and seven pairs of ears pricked in our direction. Then old Ria, our retired brood mare, and acknowledged matriarch of the paddock, took two steps forward. As if on cue from her silent command, a wave of horses began walking quietly and rhythmically towards us, with the occasional musical call that horse lovers know so well.

'What was it you said about trouble with catching?' I asked sweetly as they drew near.

One in particular began to quicken his pace. Webster, after staring intently at Ginge's bright locks, broke into a steady trot, then, unbelievably, cantered – actually cantered – towards her, reaching over the fence to snuffle at her ears.

It was a case of love at first sight.

'Isn't he bea-u-tiful!' breathed Ginge. 'I love that bright chestnut colour, he sort of matches *me*.'

'You must never choose a horse by its looks,' said her friend severely, then, turning to me, 'what's his breeding? How old is he? What's he done?'

'He's a part-bred Arab, eight years old and a good all-rounder, but a bit on the – er – lethargic side,' I said, still reeling from the surprise of Webster's enthusiastic approach. 'Depending, of course, on the skill of the rider,' I added pointedly.

'What about this one?' Ginge's friend was fondling Toss's silky ears with well-manicured fingers. 'She's a nice, compact little mare.'

'No,' Ginge was resolute. 'This is the one I want to try. Suits me if he is a bit leth – letharg – whatever you said. So am I, after a day's work and I'm not looking for the Horse of the Year. Can I try him?'

'Certainly. Here's the headcollar. Put it on him yourself.' I could not resist a look of smug satisfaction as Webster did his usual obliging dip-nose-in-loop act.

In the manège Webster's enthusiasm waned a little. He liked his new carrot-coloured friend but he hadn't expected her to want him to *work*.

Rosemary handed Ginge a riding crop. 'You might need this,' she murmured discreetly.

Ginge was a better rider than I expected, but even so, she only succeeded in getting the most muted responses from Webster. He walked amiably enough, trotted unenthusiastically and cantered only half way round each time before dropping back into his own version of a jog-trot.

'You'll have to push him on more, Sarah,' said Best Friend sharply. 'He's a bit of a slug.' Her choice of phrase was unfortunate, and Rosemary's brow darkened.

In my own irritation I noted that one little mystery had been solved. I knew Ginge's real name at last. The most determined name-clipper of her colleagues would have difficulty in reducing 'Sarah', pronounced as I had just heard it, with a short 'a', to a single syllable. 'Ginger' was much more malleable.

But Ginge alias Sarah was already in love with her new mount, and criticisms fell on deaf ears.

'Can I try jumping him? Can he jump?'

'Yes. Try that.' Rosemary was already arranging a coloured pole.

Webster came round in a circle and looked at the jump with astonished resignation before blundering his way straight through it.

'I think we've seen enough,' said Best Friend, her lips in a thin line.

'Oh no! It was my fault, really it was. I'm out of practice.' Sarah was obviously crestfallen by her friend's lack of enthusiasm.

'I think,' cut in Rosemary smoothly, 'he's just full of good grass. I'll wake him up a bit for you.'

Sarah slid ruefully to the ground to be replaced in the saddle by Rosemary, hatless and in her old jeans, but with a glint in her eye and a riding crop in her hand.

The effect was dramatic. Here was a different kettle of fish, Webster decided. The rider on his back was none other than the Giver of Feeds, Filler of Haynets, and undisputed Boss of the Stable Yard. He stepped briskly forward, broke into a rhythmic trot, performed several figures-of-eight faultlessly, executed a graceful serpentine then cleared the jumping pole as if it did not exist.

'Would you raise the jump a bit, please?' Rosemary's request was both casual and authoritative, and it was addressed directly at Best Friend. She moved forward with alacrity and added several inches to the height. Rosemary and Webster sailed over it then came to a halt at the gate.

'Now try him,' said Rosemary, and handed back the reins.

Webster had learnt his lesson. While the Boss looked on, twiddling a pigtail severely, he set to work to obey Sarah's every command, and the pair trotted, cantered and jumped in happy understanding of each other.

'There! I told you it was me!' Sarah's flushed pink cheeks glowed almost as brightly as her hair. 'Oh, I definitely want him. Can we discuss it?'

'What about traffic?' Her friend's voice was like a dash of cold water over the warmth of her enthusiasm. 'Have you thought about that?'

'He's a hundred per cent unshakeable,' I said. 'I've hacked him out myself.'

'All the same, I think she should try him out on the road before deciding. I take it you have no objections?'

I glanced at Rosemary. Both she and Marigold had had a long day, and Rosemary, I knew, had a dental appointment in less than an hour.

'I'm sorry,' I said, 'but the girls will be leaving shortly and there's no-one to accompany her. With the greatest respect I can't let her go out alone.'

'I'll accompany her,' said Best Friend coolly. 'I've given my word to her husband that I'll check every detail. I've got a hat and boots in the car.'

'I'll tack up one of the others,' Rosemary offered.

'I'd rather like to try the big Cremello.'

'I'm sorry. He's a very highly schooled horse. We never let anyone ride him unless we are absolutely sure of their ability,' was Rosemary's blunt reply.

There is something about the way an unknown rider smoothly adjusts the stirrup length, checks the girth and swings lightly into the saddle that betrays instantly the ease of long experience. Toss recognised it too. An exploratory flip of the head brought a gentle but sharp tap on the neck, and she didn't try again. As Sarah and her friend trotted out of the drive, I knew that, gamble though it was, the horses were in good hands.

With Rosemary and Marigold gone, the half hour that followed seemed an eternity. What if there *was* an accident? Was my insurance fully comprehensive? I wished desperately that I had taken more notice of the policies and not left the small print, as always, to George. I should have been firm and told them to come back when the girls were available, but Sarah was so keen and her friend such a wet blanket. And there again, perhaps *I* was the one that was being taken for a ride, giving free hacking to comparative strangers!

My thoughts were interrupted by the cheerful clip-clop of hooves returning up the drive. Both riders looked relaxed and smiling. Yes, *both* were smiling, and I found to my surprise that Best Friend had a fine set of even, white teeth.

'They were marvellous,' enthused Sarah. 'We met the lot – cars, lorries, motor-bikes – and neither of them flinched.'

'They've certainly both been very well handled,' agreed her friend, stroking Toss's sleek neck thoughtfully.

'I definitely want him.' Sarah's delight was irrepressible as they untacked the horses ready to return them to the paddock.

'Subject to a vet's certificate, of course,' said her friend firmly, and the brief smile had gone.

They could not have chosen a worse day for the veterinary examination. A high wind had howled dismally all night sending a battery of rain against the windows like bursts of gunfire. Twice George got up to batten down loose catches and close tapping doors.

In the morning the sky had an ominous damson-black look and a strange brooding atmosphere lurked behind the howl of the wind. At 10 a.m. all the lights were on in the house and we heard the first menacing growl of thunder. Suddenly the heavens seemed to split apart above us and rain poured in torrents to be driven in near-horizontal sheets by the rising gale.

Rosemary, clad from head to foot in oilskins battled her way to the back door, rain dripping from the edge of her hat and running down her pigtails.

'Surely they won't come in this,' she gasped. 'They'll have to cancel it.'

But even as she spoke the grey Porsche, phantom-like in the curtain of driving rain, appeared, moving slowly up the drive, followed by another car of darkish colour equally undistinguishable in the plum-coloured gloom. As if to announce their arrival, a blinding flash of lightning ripped across the sky to be followed by a heart-stopping crash of thunder.

Under George's enormous umbrella, I waited in the porch.

'Do you want to go on with this?' I asked Sarah and her friend as they struggled out of the car, half hidden in waterproof anoraks. 'It's an expensive business, and I can't see how it can be done satisfactorily today.'

Before they could reply we were joined by a third figure from the other car. He was a round little man. Everything about him seemed to be round: round face, round body, round spectacles; even the raindrops that quickly gathered on his coat retained their spherical perfection as they ran down to the hem, to hang like beads along the edge.

I repeated my question to him. He wiped the water from his glasses and beamed unconcernedly.

'Why not? It's as good a way as any of testing an animal's temperament,' he said.

'And the owner's temper,' I wanted to add.

In Box 1, the unsuspecting Webster was giving his full attention to the haynet. Dante's Inferno could rage around him if it wanted to, but he was inside and the hay was good. He ignored the deputation of dripping figures that invaded his privacy, some inside, some outside, leaning over the door.

The vet was slow and ponderous in his preparations, and conversation was almost impossible in the non-stop tattoo of rain on the roof.

'I'm sorry, I forgot to introduce you,' yelled Sarah above the din. 'This is Mr Weatherall.' No-one seemed to find the statement funny, least of all me.

'And what about your friend?' I shouted back. 'You never told me *her* name.'

Sarah cupped a hand round my ear. 'Barbara – Barbara Hargreaves.'

I nodded to indicate I had heard. How appropriate, I thought. Reduce *that* to one syllable and it would be apt indeed.

Mr Weatherall set about his routine inspection methodically. The door was closed temporarily while he looked closely into the astonished Webster's eyes. The heart was checked with a cold little instrument that tickled deliciously. Webster was quite enjoying all this attention, especially when all he had to do was stand still.

'I thought,' said Barbara Hargreaves in a brief lull of the noise, 'I detected signs of laminitis.'

'Never!' I screeched, outraged.

Mr Weatherall studied the hooves closely.

'Mm-m- there are a few ridges – yes – but it must have been a long time ago.'

'It's the first *I've* heard of it,' I hissed. 'No-one's ever mentioned it before. I had him vetted when I bought him.'

Mr Weatherall continued a minute inspection of Webster's sturdy legs.

'There's a small blemish on the offside rear under the fetlock,' the sharp voice cut through the drumming of the rain once again.

Another word from you, and I'll dunk your expensive cut-and-blow-dry in the water butt, I thought murderously.

'Ah yes,' agreed Mr Weatherall after several minutes of searching. 'A minor rope burn I should think,' and he made a brief note on his sheet. Then briskly, 'Now who's going to gallop him to check his wind?'

As if on cue, a crack of thunder rolled and reverberated over our heads. I looked at Rosemary. She was deathly white, and obviously dreading that she would be asked. Storms it would seem were a secret phobia. Barbara was busily searching for a handkerchief. The know-all was clearly not prepared to risk-all, not even for a friend.

'I will,' said Sarah. 'I'm the one that's got to find out and,' she laughed shakily, 'I'm paying the bill, so I'd better get my money's worth.'

8 · Tosca

The manège it seemed was not big enough, it would have to be the open paddock. I was beginning to wonder whether behind Mr Weatherall's bland, rotund appearance there lurked a touch of the hidden sadist.

The rain and wind continued unabated and patches of the ground were fast becoming a muddy quagmire.

Rosemary handed her riding crop up to a pale but resolute Sarah.

'Take him quietly to the far end, then ask him to pick up speed *on the way back*,' I heard her advise urgently. 'That should be enough.'

In no time at all, Webster was a sorry sight, wet and bedraggled, his rider equally so. The driving downpour repeatedly sent them teetering off-balance, as he tried to argue some sense into his new friend about the sheer stupidity of going for a hack on such a day. Finally they reached the far end, and turned to come home. I saw Sarah give him a sharp whack with the crop, and sure enough, Webster, on the assumption that his young rider had seen sense at last, broke into a hearty, relieved gallop. They reached us in a flurry of splattered mud, and literally skidded to a halt.

'Will that do?' gasped Sarah, flushed and triumphant behind the smears across her face.

'Just once again,' said Mr Weatherall unperturbed. 'You're doing very well.'

Without a word, Sarah turned the reluctant Webster back towards the open field. This time he fought her, the bit, the wind and the rain all the way, trying hard to turn left, turn right, swing back, anything but go forward.

'He's very nappy, isn't he?' said a cool voice at my side.

'Wouldn't you be?' I snapped back. 'On a day like this!'

At long last the two figures had reached the far end of the paddock for the second time, almost completely obscured by the curtain of rain. As they turned, a flash of lightning illuminated them clearly and Webster shot forward to a dramatic drum roll of thunder as if the devil himself were at his heels. Sarah was wisely leaning forward, jockey fashion, when yet a second flash split the gloom. Webster's hind legs flew into the air, and Sarah catapulted forwards to hang, desperately clinging upside down, under his neck.

They slithered to a stop beside us, and Sarah flopped to the sodden ground, a streak of blood at the corner of her mouth.

'It's all right,' she said shakily, wiping it with the back of a muddy hand, 'I think I've bitten my lip.'

'What happened – did he lose his balance?' Rosemary was obviously trying to keep matters low key.

'No, it was definitely a buck,' said Sarah's best friend, 'and a pretty dangerous onc at that.'

We stood in silence while Mr Weatherall applied his stethoscope to the spattered ribs. I was speechless. In all the time I had known the faithful Webster, I had never once seen him buck.

It was a bedraggled group that trailed its way back to the stable yard. With the usual perversity of British weather, the rain began to ease off as they led the miserable Webster back to his box.

'Is that it then?' I was trying hard to sound cheerful and unconcerned, and ignore the nagging pain down my right side. What was that old wives' tale about damp getting into the bones?

'Not quite.' Mr Weatherall wiped his spectacles for the umpteenth time, and made more notes. 'We have to wait a few minutes now to check any swelling in the legs.'

I was suddenly desperate for a comforting drink discreetly assisted by a couple of my pain-killer tablets.

'Do come into the kitchen, and we'll all have a coffee,' I suggested, signalling to Rosemary to join Marigold in their own comforting brew.

The moment I opened the door I regretted the invitation. I had completely forgotten that it was Mrs B's 'floor day', and our quarry-tiled kitchen floor was her pride and joy. 'Cleanliness is next to Godliness' was one of her favourite maxims, to which she invariably added, 'And getting down on your knees to give a floor a good scrub is the next best thing to praying.' As four pairs of muddy feet squelched their way over the rosy, gleaming surface it seemed sacrilege indeed.

I switched on the electric kettle and wondered bleakly why there were only three coffee mugs on the hooks. I would have to use the old discarded one for myself, hoping no-one would notice its unhygienic chip.

'It'll have to be Instant,' I said with false brightness. 'We haven't much time. How do you all like it?'

Mr Weatherall wanted his white with sugar (two spoons, please), Sarah preferred black with no sugar, and her friend was terribly sorry but she was allergic to coffee, but would appreciate a cup of tea if it wasn't too much trouble.

It was Sarah who noticed that as I juggled with the various permutations I was virtually standing on one leg.

'Oh, I'm so sorry to put you to all this trouble.' She rose, scattering mud-drops in every direction. 'Let me help.'

'The biscuit tin's in that cupboard,' I murmured and remembered a fraction too late the shopping list waiting for attention next day.

Sarah opened the tin to reveal two unhappy broken biscuits huddled together for consolation at the bottom of the cavernous emptiness. Mr Weatherall declined as he was writing his notes but 'wouldn't say no' to another cup of coffee. Sarah shook her head in defence of her waistline and Barbara wondered if she might be allowed to smoke.

I nodded dumbly. Neither George nor I smoked, and the only ashtray we possessed usually lurked somewhere between the dining-room and sitting-room as a gesture of good will to misguided guests. I traipsed through in search of it, leaving a damp trail on Mrs B's immaculate floors, and managed to return just as Mr Weatherall was gulping his last mouthful of coffee and rising to his feet.

'Fifteen minutes,' he said. 'That should do,' and gathered up his notes.

Barbara stubbed out her cigarette in the ashtray still in my hand, and we all trooped out again. My own mug of coffee sat, lukewarm and untouched, on the draining board, with two Distalgesic tablets in a teaspoon nearby.

Once again Rosemary led the disconsolate Webster out into the yard and waited, stony-faced, for instructions. By now the wind had dropped considerably and only the clouds scudding across the sky reminded us of the recent maelstrom.

Mr Weatherall examined Webster's legs yet again, made quiet clucking noises with his tongue and added a few more notes to his dissertation.

'Trot him away from me across the concrete,' he ordered, and squatted on his haunches like an aborigine about his business. He was immediately joined by Barbara, squatting likewise. Her voice rose clearly above the clip-clop of hooves.

'I fancy he's brushing a bit, isn't he?'

Mr Weatherall puckered his brows with concentration.

'N-n-o, I don't think so – and yet – perhaps you're right – er – mm-m – no – feathers need trimming a bit, that's all.'

I turned to Sarah, standing beside me.

'Is Barbara, your friend, qualified?' I asked fighting to keep the rising irritation out of my voice.

'Oh yes.' Sarah was watching the two intently. 'She used to be a riding instructress but now she's married with two children. Poor Barb, I think she misses it a bit.'

I smiled grimly to myself at the abbreviation.

Finally Mr Weatherall snapped his notebook shut and solemnly secured it with a rubber band.

'That will be all,' he said, then to Sarah, 'I'll get this typed out in the morning and if you come to the surgery about lunchtime it should be ready. I'd better be off now. I've spent longer than usual on this case and I'm running late.'

I could well believe it.

'I'll be in touch,' called Sarah as she and her friend fastened their safety belts and prepared to leave. Did I detect a slight tightness in the usual cheery smile? Barbara Hargreaves merely nodded politely as they moved away.

'That's the end of that,' I thought miserably and turned back to the house.

Suddenly a ray of bright golden light pierced the clouds and bathed the whole damp scene in a benevolent glow. I raised my fist to the watery sun in its solitary patch of blue.

'You blithering idiot!' I yelled in a paroxysm of frustration, pain and disappointment. 'You're too darned late!'

Mrs B leaning out of a bedroom window dropped her duster and her jaw in astonishment.

'You'd better come inside,' she said, 'And I'll make you a nice cup of tea.'

I had just finished my scrambled eggs on toast the following lunchtime, and was settling down to another gothic helping of *The Woman in White* when the telephone rang. It was several seconds before I could disentangle from the excited, incoherent babbling at the other end either the caller or the message. By dint of some rapid linguistic and phonetic manipulation I pieced together the jigsaw.

It was Ginge – sorry – Sarah. Derek said she could definitely have him – Webster not Derek – (giggle). She was lucky really, he was such a darling – Derek not Webster – but *he* was a darling too! She would give in her notice tomorrow – no, it would have to be the next day – *that* would give them something to talk about. They'll probably all think she's pregnant (giggle). Could they please, please, PLEASE come over later in the afternoon to settle it. She was *so* excited, and wasn't it all marvellous?

I gulped and tried to gather my wits.

'What about the vet's report. Was it all right?'

'Oh fine. Mr Weatherall says he's as sound as a bell – no problem.'

'You weren't worried about that buck then?'

'No, you couldn't blame *him*. I nearly shot out of my shirt myself with that second flash. Mr Weatherall says any other horse would have bolted like hell.'

I refrained from observing that to my knowledge, bolting like hell never had been, and never would be, part of Webster's repertoire.

'Please can we come over when I've finished work today to settle it? There's something I specially want to ask you.'

I wasn't too sure about that last bit. It had a familiar ring, but I was caught up in her enthusiasm.

'All right. I'll look forward to seeing you both between five and six.'

I had assumed that the 'we' would be Sarah and the unknown Derek. I was wrong. As the grey Porsche turned into the drive for the third time, I had already guessed what to expect as Sarah and Barbara emerged, the latter clad in elegant jodhpurs and boots, as was Sarah.

In the sitting-room, they sat on the edge of their chairs and looked at each other as if waiting for a cue.

'I don't know where to begin,' said Sarah smiling nervously. 'The fact is . . . the fact is . . .'

'Is it a money problem?' I prompted. That after all, was the usual run of things.

'Yes, well, no – not exactly. Oh, I don't know how to put it.'

Barbara was fumbling for a cigarette. I pushed the ashtray towards her.

'Do relax, Ginge,' I said and the old familiar name slipped out before I could stop it. 'Start at the beginning. We're old acquaintances. Just pop all the problems into an imaginary trolley and I'll try and wheel them away!'

My use of her nickname seemed to give her courage. She leaned back in her chair and took a deep breath.

'Well, Derek says I can have Webster, and the fact is – well – Barb wants to know if you'll sell her Toss as well.'

I had an uncomfortable feeling of *déjà vu* and images of Penny Williams flickered through my mind. Was there something odd about Toss that she got involved in this sort of situation? Perhaps, true to her Highland ancestry, she was 'fey'.

I looked at Barbara who exhaled a thin thread of blue smoke and then smiled, showing the even white teeth I had seen so briefly when she returned from her hack. What a pity I thought that she didn't smile more often – it transformed the cool, patrician features completely.

She opened her mouth to speak, but Sarah rushed on, the words tumbling out over each other.

'You see, Barb's just moved into a new house and it's got two loose boxes and a paddock, and I'm going to keep Webster there, and Barb feels he ought to have a stable companion, and she's been looking for a young horse to bring on anyway, and it would be such a useful arrangement. We could take it in turns to do the mucking out and exercising for each other, and I'd get professional help, and oh, it would be just perfect!'

'There's the question of price,' I addressed Barbara. 'Toss is part-bred like Webster but with a Highland dam instead of Welsh, and she's quite green as yet. I take it you'll want Mr

Weatherall to check her too?'

'Oh no, that won't be necessary. Sarah's husband engaged my help in a professional capacity, although we are friends . . .'

'Barb's husband's an accountant and mine's a mechanic,' cut in Sarah. 'We do their cars and they do our accounts.'

'. . . and I was under obligation to be thorough. But in my case I can afford to take a risk – not that I think there *is* a risk,' she added hastily. 'I took the liberty of checking her over when I returned her to the paddock the other day. And she's absolutely perfect on the road.' She thought for a few seconds. 'I'm prepared to offer the same price as for Webster if that is acceptable to you.'

'And that's the next awkward bit,' said Sarah anxiously. She delved into a large plastic bag to produce a smaller one of the kind all too familiar at her check-out counter. With a single movement she turned it upside down and a deluge of notes fell out over the coffee table and on the carpet.

'There's four hundred pounds there, and Barb's got some more.'

Barbara in turn produced a large brown package from her handbag and carefully placed a perfect fan-shape of notes on the table beside the untidy pile, much in the manner of a card-sharper displaying his hand.

'Another four hundred,' said Sarah, her voice shaking slightly. 'We wondered . . . we wondered . . . as we're buying two, if you would accept it as deposits and let us pay the balance at a hundred pounds on the first of each month.'

Before I could reply in my astonishment Barbara had searched in her handbag again and produced two sheets of typewritten paper.

'I know it's a lot to ask,' she explained, 'so I've taken the liberty of having two agreements drawn up for your approval. We really are a bit tight, cash-wise, at the moment. I've just moved house, and Sarah's Derek's just started up his business. But, of course, if you're not agreeable we'll quite understand.'

The two sheets were identical except for the names, and it

was immediately apparent that Barbara's accountant husband included a pet solicitor among his clientèle. Each statement agreed to pay a deposit of four hundred pounds in cash and the balance of (blank) at the rate of one hundred pounds per calendar month, payable on the first of each month. The statements also dealt with such relevant matters as shoeing, veterinary fees, insurance against accident or death, and promised to provide 'such care and feeding as deemed necessary by the owner' until the final amount was paid.

One was signed by Sarah Gunther (Mrs) and the other by Barbara Avril Hargreaves (Mrs) in the presence of two witnesses, each supplying addresses and telephone numbers. At the bottom of each sheet was also a codicil-type P.S. The above named was prepared to buy the complete tack of the animal concerned, if available, at a price to be agreed, in cash, on completion of the selling price.

A space at the end was marked with two pencil crosses and the request 'please sign'. My own address was already neatly typed in.

There was total silence as I read the sheets, except for a slight cough from Barbara over her cigarette.

'Won't they do?' Sarah's voice was thin and childlike.

'I don't know what to say,' I replied with total truth. 'I think, if you'll excuse me, I'll give my husband a ring.'

Inevitably George was not at his extension. All our married life I had noticed this phenomenon. If I merely wanted to contact him with a request to pick up an extra pint of milk on his way home, he would answer immediately. But if it was a matter of extreme importance or anxiety, he was invariably at some remote part of the establishment, apparently light years away from the nearest telephone.

'Actually,' said the switchboard girl briskly. 'It's just on five-thirty. He's probably left, knowing what the traffic's like. I've got my coat on myself.'

I could have kicked myself for my stupidity. Of course, George would have started his thirty mile journey back, and it would be some time before he reached home 'knowing what the traffic was like'.

I hovered in the hall to delay my return to the sitting-room. Should I say I would think about it and tell them to come back? Or make what businessmen were fond of calling a 'snap decision'? On my last visit to the hospital the consultant had advised that, after such a prolonged period of enforced inactivity, I should now start taking positive steps to ease myself back into some active pursuit or other, and keep myself mentally alert.

Right! So I would be mentally alert. Bearing in mind Ginge's many little kindnesses to me in my early, wobbly days at the supermarket, and Barbara's obviously knowledgeable background with horses, plus the fact that Webster and Toss were doomed to lazy deterioration in the paddocks if not given regular work, and . . . where was I? Oh yes, I was being mentally alert. All things considered, there must be *some* honest people in the world, not to mention, of course, eight hundred pounds lying on the coffee table and carpet at that very minute. Yes, I would make a snap decision.

I returned to the girls with a surprisingly firm tread.

'All right, girls,' I said, 'you've got yourself a deal.'

I was nearly knocked headlong off my newly acquired firm tread, as Sarah shot up from her armchair and threw her arms round my neck.

'Oh, I *knew* you would,' she gasped, unashamedly brushing away a surge of tears, while I, recovering my composure somewhat shakily, wondered how many horse deals had been clinched with a fervent kiss.

Barbara in her turn gave one of her fleeting smiles, except that this time it stayed.

'You won't regret it,' she said. 'And you'll be very welcome to call any time you like to see how they are.'

With all the appropriate blanks filled in and signatures completed there now remained the question of when the horses could be removed.

'Oh,' said Sarah, her eyes still pink-rimmed with emotion, 'we thought – we thought we would hack them back now, if you'll lend us the tack.'

'But there's no-one to get them ready.'

'That's all right. We'll do it *all*, catch them, brush them off, tack them up. Oh, I can't wait!'

Half an hour later two smart riders on two smart horses clip-clopped happily down the drive, a pearl grey Porsche stood abandoned by the front door and I paid a furtive visit to the brandy bottle.

'You've WHAT?' roared George on his return, and the china ornaments on the bookcase actually rattled.

'But they've signed agreements, *and* left eight hundred pounds, and the car with the ignition key in it,' I quavered. Suddenly the business of being mentally alert after hours under the anaesthetic, weeks on crutches, and months leaning on a stick, had taken on the dimension of an ascent of Mount Everest.

George read the agreements carefully.

'Mm-m,' he murmured grudgingly. 'Everything seems to be covered quite satisfactorily, I must say.'

He counted the eight hundred pounds with slow deliberation.

'You can see what's happened here,' he added, voicing my own private thoughts. 'The grateful Derek has given his wife the full amount for Webster in return for her unpaid services in the new business, and she's shared it with her friend to secure both animals.' He glanced at the calendar, somewhat mollified by the wad of notes in his hand. 'Ah well, seventeen days from now you'll know whether it was a Good Deal or a Good-bye to the balance.'

Those seventeen days seemed endless. The grey Porsche disappeared from the drive after two young mechanics arrived with a note of authority but not before George had sneaked a test-drive 'to keep the battery from going flat'.

Ginge also disappeared from Check-out Three and was replaced by a pert little miss with a snub nose whose name, I was not surprised to hear, was Steph.

September 1st finally arrived bright and full of hope as did the postman, with a postcard from a friend holidaying in Benidorm and an invitation to win a fortune from one of several lucky numbers if I bought my thermal underwear within fourteen days.

'Well,' I suggested tremulously, 'if they *send* it on the first, it won't reach us till the second, will it?' and was bleakly reminded of the lengthy hours of studying the excuses made by one Troilus over his missing Cressida in long off college days.

The following morning the drive was blank and empty at post-time and George departed for work with a set face, and a curious expression in his eyes which alternated between pity and you-should-have-known-better.

At eleven o'clock Mrs B wandered in with a large beige envelope in her hand.

'The little boy from the farm just gave me this,' she said vaguely, 'I think it's been put through the wrong door,' and must have wondered at the avid eagerness with which I pounced on it.

Inside the large envelope there were two smaller ones. The first, in thin business-type manilla, contained one hundred pounds in crossed postal orders and a hastily written note.

Dear Mrs Melrose,

This is the first £100 as promised. Hope the P.O's are O.K. Same again next month. Derek thinks Webster is grate.

Love,

Sarah.

XX

P.S. Hope your feeling better now.

The second envelope was thick, oblong and dark blue. It contained a cheque for one hundred pounds signed with Barbara's flourish and a short typed letter.

Dear Mrs Melrose,

Herewith the first hundred pounds as agreed, the balance to follow.

Tosca has settled down very well indeed and is showing great promise both on the flat and over coloured jumps.

I do hope you won't mind the change of name but she has already lost that little habit, and, of course, it will sound better when I enter her for the various classes at local shows (although I think her potential will take her far beyond that level).

Thank you once again for your kind help and co-operation.

Yours sincerely,

Barbara A. Hargreaves

'Yippee!' I yelled, giving Mrs B a bear-hug as she passed by with an armful of washing. 'There *are* some honest people in the world after all!'

'Ug,' she gulped, retrieving an air-borne pillow slip, 'if you can find them.'

At Christmas we all three exchanged Christmas cards. I beat the seasonal rush (and saved postage) by enclosing receipts for 'full and final payment' in both of mine.

9 · Desert Sand

I sat bolt upright, all my senses and nerves alert. The bedroom was murky black, and the only sound above the thudding of my own heart was the distant poing-poing of a dripping tap. A vague amber glow from the window turned the comforting familiarity of the bedroom furniture into grotesque menacing shapes. Could it be fire in the stable yard? But there was no flickering, only a weird, waiting stillness.

Not a sound came from George's room next door where he slept, still exiled, since my accident. What had awakened me, clear-headed and alert so suddenly? The whole house was silent. If an intruder had entered we would certainly have heard by now. Downstairs, Mamie, our old bull terrier, would not entertain an inquisitive mouse, let alone an uninvited human, and the stairs and landing were well supplied with loudly protesting creaking boards. 'Best burglar alarms in the business,' George had said, 'and the cheapest.' So why this wide awake tension, this feeling of an unseen presence making my palms sweat?

Slowly I edged over the bed and fished for my slippers with my good leg. The scrape of their soles on the carpet sounded thunderous to my overstrung nerves. I slipped through the door and nearly dropped with shock at the tearing, grinding moan that greeted me – the loose floorboards were doing their job. Any stranger in the house would most certainly know they had been discovered, and what use was I, leaning on the wall without my stick?

Trembling, I eased George's door open – comfort and reassurance lay beyond it – and leaned over to shake him as quietly as I could.

The bedcover was smooth, the sheets and pillows cool and unruffled. His bed had not been slept in, and the luminous dial on the bedside clock said 2.25 a.m. I had been awakened by an awareness not of a presence but an absence. The stillness of the empty house was suddenly suffocating.

For several weeks now we had slipped into a pleasant routine. Once I was tucked up in bed, usually early and with a good book, George would do his final rounds, checking the horses and padlocked gates, installing the cats in the feed room and taking Mamie for her last walk.

I had always been uneasy about the paddock-checking routine, as it involved a solitary walk through the shadowy secretiveness of the spinney. But George had only laughed. He knew every bush and every tree better than any intruder, he said, and always carried a stout stick. Nevertheless, I usually tried to stay awake until I heard his reassuring footsteps back in the kitchen. But this time I had fallen asleep.

Was he lying out there injured, either by accident or attack? Was the intruder – it – still lurking there waiting for my feeble investigation? And why was the dog so silent?

Better not put the light on and give my presence away. Furtively I groped for my stick and started an unsteady descent of the stairs, gripping the bannisters hard. But a cacophony of sound, deafening in the background of silence, accompanied me. Wailing, screeching, groaning, each step proclaimed to any waiting ear that I was on my way down.

At the bottom, a knife-edge gleam stabbed the darkness. The lights were still on behind the kitchen door, and with them, our faithful old Mamie, strangely silent.

Sick with apprehension I turned the handle and peered in. The room was empty and an untouched mug of Ovaltine, a worried wrinkle of skin on its surface, stood by the sink. Mamie rose from her basket sleepily surprised but in no way agitated.

'Mamie,' I whispered urgently, 'where's Master?'

She was instantly alert. That was a word she knew and loved. She thumped a languid tail and gazed intently at the window. One mystery at least was solved; the curtains were still wide apart and the bright kitchen light, reflected on the concrete terrace outside, had been the source of the amber glow that suffused dimly into the bedroom. Beyond the terrace, a necklace of gleaming pin-points told that the pilot lights in the stable yard were still on too.

Mamie's homely bulk and sleepy-dog smell were instantly comforting. Of course! There must be something amiss with the horses and George, conscientious as always, was dealing with it on the spot. Colic maybe? I grabbed a warm duffel coat from behind the door, pushed my pyjama-clad legs into gumboots and clipped on Mamie's lead.

'Come on, old girl,' I said, 'maybe Master needs help!'

Away from the bright cheer of the kitchen my courage waned. The herbaceous border and several tall, ornamental bushes had to be negotiated before I reached the stable yard. Mamie too, seemed uneasy and kept close to my legs, her rotund body hampering my progress.

As we passed a young conifer, a silent, shadowy shape flitted across my face to be followed by another brushing over my hair, and I stifled a cry.

I had once found an abandoned baby bat lying helpless in the feed room, and, intrigued by its beady black eyes and tiny snub nose had wondered how such a quaint little creature had acquired its sinister, Draculean notoriety. Now I knew. In the darkness their silent swooping was both uncanny and unnerving. 'All I need now,' I thought shakily, 'is the gothic hoot of an owl,' and nearly dropped with dread as that very sound drifted to me eerily from the skeleton of our ancient, dying elm.

Both dog and human reached Box 1 with relief. Mamie sat down silently while I peered into the dim interior, lit only by the pilot-light on the overhang outside.

Since Toss – alias Tosca's – departure, we had gradually accustomed the lonely Pitch to sleeping there each night. Being nearest to the house he seemed to gain some comfort from the general comings and goings. For days he had called and called for his sister, restlessly pacing up and down the paddock fence, until at least one neighbour had 'wondered what was the matter with that poor horse, and had we seen a vet?' The calling stopped, but the unhappy pacing continued in the box often well into the night.

But tonight all was quiet. Pitch was snuggled in his straw, forelegs comfortably bent beneath him, sound asleep. I strained my eyes as they became accustomed to the gloom and my heart missed a beat. In the far corner a figure was huddled, slumped against the wall and half hidden in the banked-up straw. Even without seeing the face I knew it was George. As I fumbled with the safety catch, endless possibilities rushed through my head: not least of them – had the unhappy young gelding finally given vent to his frustration in a well aimed, lethal kick?

Once inside, Mamie stood stock still for a few terrible seconds, rigidly tense, then rushed forward with wagging tail to lick a dimly visible ear beneath the turned-up collar.

'George!' I cried frantically, as the gelding struggled bewildered to his feet. 'GEORGE!'

'Mm-m? Yes? What?'

I was so relieved to hear his voice that my own sounded unnaturally high-pitched and sharp.

'What *are* you doing here? It's very late!'

'Mm-m – eh? Must have dozed off. Thought I'd keep the poor little beggar company till he settled down.'

He scrambled to his feet stiffly, brushing straw from his jacket and hair, and yawned.

'It's quite warm in the straw,' he said. 'I'd no idea it could be so comfortable. Have I missed the late News?'

From that night onwards, George was Pitch's god (while I was guilty of insubordination, refusing point blank to retire until the last round of the paddocks and stables was done).

Each day Pitch tolerated the company of his four-legged acquaintances in the paddock, but long before George's car was due in the drive, he would take up his stand at the gate and wait, motionless, with ears pricked, for the very first sound of the engine. Gradually a little ritual was evolved. George would park the car, have a preliminary cup of tea, then walk quietly through the spinney to be greeted with an ecstasy of whinnies and snuffles, and the sort of exuberant welcome more often associated with a puppy than a horse. Had it been within the range of equine capabilities he most certainly would have wagged his tail.

This was followed by a secret little treat: a slice of carrot or – delight of delights – a Polo mint furtively extracted from a hip pocket. They both knew that Bossy Pigtails of the stable yard strongly disapproved, something to do with titbits encouraging bad habits, but what could *she* know of the comradeship of a juicy apple, carefully sliced with a secret penknife and shared between a horse and his Man? They would stand quietly together, the horse peacefully chomping on his treat, the man feeling the frustrations and anxieties of the day unwind themselves away, as ink-stained fingers lingered caressingly along the glossy mane.

They walked side by side back through the spinney to the comfort and welcome of the stable, where the water was always fresher, the feed tastier, the straw more inviting if prepared by George's hand alone. And as for the ultimate stable companion – guess who?

As the weeks passed, however, Rosemary began to show a

growing concern. Pitch was over four years old now, lightly backed but otherwise unschooled. The puppy-ish exuberance in George's presence all too often deteriorated into a wayward naughtiness when he was not around; and once or twice, even in George's company he had found the spinney an ideal place for a bit of skittish nonsense.

Rosemary also had another problem – our last working pupil had gone. Asked if she would be good enough to rinse out the two coffee mugs as she was preparing to leave at 5.55 p.m., Marigold had airily remarked that 'it would make her late'. Rosemary had replied with some exasperation that she, Marigold, had taken over half an hour to drink the former contents in what was supposed to be a fifteen minutes' break.

'Well,' huffed Marigold, 'if you're going to be *Victorian* about it, counting every second it takes to drink a cup of coffee, you can keep your job,' and walked out, never to return.

'Funnily enough,' remarked Rosemary later, 'it's actually easier without her. By the time I had explained what I wanted, then stood over her to make sure she did it properly, it would have been quicker to do it myself.'

Nevertheless, she still had five horses to care for, with little time for systematic schooling and exercising, and young Pitch was showing signs of becoming a handful.

'It's a pity you can't ride,' she said to George one day. 'That youngster would go through fire and water for you. Would you like to learn?'

But George shook his head. 'I wouldn't have enough time to do you or him justice,' he said with genuine regret, 'but I agree, a solution will have to be found.'

The solution came in the form of young Trevor Apsley. Trevor was a neighbour who had taken lessons with us before my accident – a youngster remarkable, not so much for actual ability, but for the enthusiasm with which he tried everything. Now, having left school, like so many of his age group he was kicking his heels in the dole queue.

One day, out of sheer boredom, he 'just dropped in' to see

how I was recovering and whether there were still any horses about. He had, in fact, been one of our most promising young riders, but had found out, like many of his contemporaries that riding elsewhere was a costly business.

As he chatted to Rosemary he automatically held open the haynets for her to fill them, then tied them expertly to their rings.

'You know,' said Rosemary thoughtfully after he had gone, 'Trevor was a real help today. I've got an idea. He seems to have time on his hands, and he was always good with the horses, would you be agreeable to letting him come on a daily basis? He could ride and give a hand in return for free riding lessons. He's keen to learn and it wouldn't affect his Social Security, or whatever it is he gets paid. I'd be happy to teach him.'

I put the idea to George that evening and he was surprisingly enthusiastic.

'Why not? Everybody will gain. He'll get free lessons, Rosemary will get free help, and Pitch will get some much-needed discipline.'

The scheme was an instant success. Each day Trevor arrived, incongruous in full riding gear on his bicycle, and ready to give a hand at anything in return for the much prized riding lessons.

'In fact,' said Rosemary happily, 'he's so enthusiastic he's in danger of becoming a fanatic!'

Pitch wasn't *too* sure at first about this hefty youngster taking command on his back. He was used to Bossy Pigtails sitting there lightly, doing odd things with her heels, or even hanging on to the other end of a lunge rein, but this fellow was sometimes a shade too domineering. But then, his beloved George himself had introduced them, and even adjusted the stirrups once or twice, so it must be all right.

Soon he began to enjoy the routine; it filled in the gap nicely till George came home in the evening. And this young rider showed him such interesting things, with Bossy Pigtails always standing around having her say, of course. They walked and trotted and even cantered, making funny shapes in the manège

– big circles, small circles, figures of eight and sometimes they actually jumped over some brightly coloured trees that must have fallen on the ground. Now *that* really was something! He liked it best of all, and sometimes had to be stopped from over enthusiasm. Once or twice he bashed straight through and Bossy Pigtails got very cross and made them go straight back and do it again. Another time, when he lost his nerve a bit, his young rider actually fell off. But he stood absolutely still so that he could get back up with dignity – it was the least a fellow could do.

Other times they went through the gate to the Big Outside and along the lane where the shiny monsters with four wheels instead of legs roared up and down. He did not like that so much. One day a baby monster, still with only two wheels, came up behind him suddenly, making too much noise as youngsters will, and buzzed him like an enormous wasp. He was so startled he shot smartly into a hedge. His young rider seemed to be as scared as he was – his sweat-smell got very strong. Anyway, they both came back to the paddock as soon as they could.

But all in all, the days were pretty good. Plenty of games and work with his energetic new friend during the daytime, and in the evening his secret treats and quiet times with George. What more could a young horse want?

Rosemary, too, was pleased.

'They're both making very good progress,' she reported. 'I don't normally approve of young riders on green horses, but these two seem to understand each other; they're both keen. In fact, sometimes they're both *too* keen,' and she glanced with satisfaction at the row of water buckets already filled.

One day Trevor tapped at the kitchen door as he was due to leave, and cleared his throat nervously. He was a large, bulky boy with an uncongruously baby face well bespattered with freckles.

'Mum says will it be all right if she pops round some time tomorrow?'

'Of course. When would she like to come?'

'About eleven, to watch me ride. Then she'd like to talk to you.'

'Good. Tell her I'll look forward to seeing her then.'

That was not strictly true. I knew Mrs Apsley of old. A lady of voluptuous proportions, she had a somewhat bizarre taste in lipstick, nail varnish and eye-shadow, and was apt to attend the local Parent–Teacher occasions with an excess of cleavage and chatter.

I was not, however, prepared for the spectacle that presented itself the following day.

A white Jaguar purred to a halt, complete with simulated leopard-skin seat covers, and a platinum blonde stepped out. Enormous hazel eyes blinked glassily behind newly acquired contact lenses, their watery rims spoiling the elaborate eye make-up.

'My DEAR Mrs Melrose. How ARE you? How DO you keep so slim? No, don't answer that. You've had SUCH a terrible time – we've heard ALL about it. No WONDER you've lost so much weight!'

(If, in her skin-tight jeans and triple ear studs she was trying to look like her son's elder sister she had ALMOST succeeded!)

Together we watched Trevor and Pitch go through their little display in the manège. Rosemary had worked well on them both, and each had gained confidence and experience from the other. The boy made up for any lapses of skill with a touch of his mother's flamboyance, and Pitch was game to try anything and everything asked of him.

Already I knew what the question would be. With Trevor out of work – so DEPRESSING for all these youngsters – it would be a MARVELLOUS opportunity for him to do some serious competing, and, of course, SHE would love to join in and help. Staying at home was SUCH a bore, especially now they had an au pair. An absolute TREASURE she was. Didn't have to be TOLD – just got on with it. SWEDISH you know.

One and a half hours of non-stop gush later I managed to

persuade her that it was George's decision really, as he was very fond of that particular pony, and he would ring her that evening.

George was very quiet when I explained the new developments, and spent longer than usual in Box 1 where Pitch was now regularly installed after his day's activities with Trevor, thus cutting out the companionable walk through the spinney.

'We have to be sensible,' he said at last, after an elaborate pretence of listening to the nine o'clock news. 'He needs a rider now. Young Trevor handles him well, and obviously thinks the world of him.'

One hour later it was settled. They would pick Pitch up the next morning, and, since they were old acquaintances in a sense, George would break his usual rule and accept a cheque. He put the receiver down slowly, selected a large red apple from the bowl, and went out to the stable yard without another word.

The three of us were in Box 1 with Pitch when they arrived. To nobody's surprise George had personally taken on the ritual of Pitch's final grooming.

He looked up, hoof-oil brush in hand, as the platinum blonde head appeared over the door.

'Ah! THERE you are! I've brought the cheque. Doesn't he look BEA-U-TIFUL!'

Expressionless, George took the cheque in an oily hand, glanced at the elaborate, showy signature, then stuffed it into his pocket.

Trevor's head now joined his mother's over the stable door, each freckle seeming to radiate anticipation.

'We wondered,' said Mrs Apsley lighting a cigarette and leaning a leather-clad elbow on the No Smoking sign, 'whether you would do us a VERY great favour, and lend us his tack for just a FEW days. We want to get it copied exactly – BRAND NEW, of course.'

'Certainly,' George's voice was muffled from somewhere in the region of Pitch's tail. 'Get his tack, Rosemary, will you?'

'Oh it's all right. Trevor will get it. He knows where it is. Come on, Trev, tack up your OWN HORSE!'

Trevor's head disappeared, and George's loomed up over Pitch's withers.

'Tack him up? That won't be necessary in a horse-box, the headcollar is enough. I suggest you put the tack in the car.'

'Oh, we haven't brought a HORSE-box. Trevor is going to HACK him over to the livery yard. It's only four miles.'

'Which way?' There was a sudden tension in the atmosphere. Rosemary glanced at me with startled eyes.

'Just up the lane to the roundabout, then STRAIGHT down the High Street – the shortest way.'

'You can't do that!' George was aghast. 'He's only a youngster. He's never been in heavy traffic before. The High Street's very narrow and much too busy, especially on a Saturday.'

'It'll be all right. Trevor's HAD him out on the road, and he said he was MARVELLOUS. Anyway, I'm going to ESCORT them all the way with the Jag.'

'Why not a brass band?' I thought numbly. Rosemary, never one to intervene unless asked, obviously thought that this was a moment that demanded some clear-headed professionalism.

'A young horse has to be taken on slowly, Mrs Apsley, so as to keep his confidence. Pitch is still green, and the High Street with all those pedestrian crossings and buses could frighten him badly. It's not as if Trevor is very experienced himself. There could be a serious accident.'

Mrs Apsley regarded her coldly, and ground out her cigarette in silence as Trevor re-appeared with bridle and saddle.

'Pop them on,' she said to her son, 'We MUST get going soon. They're waiting at the livery stables, and they're VERY particular.'

I found my voice, and suddenly it was that of the college principal addressing a difficult parent once again.

'I'm sorry, Mrs Apsley,' I said in measured tones, 'but I cannot permit this animal to leave the premises under those conditions.'

She looked me straight in the face.

'You can't STOP us,' she said with the slightest hint of a smirk. 'He's OUR HORSE now – we've paid for him.'

In the incredible silence that followed, George opened the stable door, handing Pitch's lead rein to Rosemary with an unspoken command, and systematically placed the dandy brush, the body brush, the curry comb, the hoof pick and the oil jar in their respective places with elaborate care and precision. Trevor stood stock still, his back arched with the weight of the saddle and bridle. Mrs Apsley, temporarily non-plussed by this unexpected display of routine activity at such a moment, waited with a be-ringed hand on one hip.

George dusted some horse hairs from his trousers then felt in his pocket. Slowly he extracted the folded cheque and thrust it into Mrs Apsley's free hand.

'Today is Saturday, Mrs Apsley. I can't pay this cheque in till Monday, and it won't be cleared until Wednesday. Until the cash is in my hands, Pitch is still my wife's horse. And as of now – HE IS NO LONGER FOR SALE.' He stooped to pick up a fallen broom. 'Now if you will excuse us, we're rather busy.'

Less than an hour later, during lunch, the telephone rang.

'Ignore it,' growled George. 'You know who that'll be.'

It rang again ten minutes later, then ten minutes after that. After the sixth unanswered call I grew desperate.

'George, for heaven's sake answer it. It could be something serious. Either that, or they'll badger us for the rest of the day.'

'You answer it,' he said gruffly. 'I can't trust myself to be civil.'

'Five-one-three-four?'

'Is that Mrs Melrose?'

'Yes?'

'This is Mr Apsley. Could I speak to your husband please?'

I had met Mr Apsley, a self-made, quiet little man, a builder by trade, he was refreshingly unconcerned about his modest origins.

'I'm sorry, he's not available at the moment. Can I give him a message?'

'Well – yes. Will you tell him I've had a long talk with the wife, and told her you're quite right. Used to do a bit of ridin' myself once, in the army, so I know a thing or two. She's gone to bed with one of her headaches, but wants me to give her apologies. Trevor's been cryin' his eyes out; thinks the world of that horse, he does, and he's come on a treat with your Rosemary, so . . .' He cleared his throat noisily. 'I could probably get a horse-box over to you this afternoon. That is, if you'll be good enough to accept the wife's apologies. She just got carried away a bit.'

'I think I can hear my husband coming. You'd better speak to him,' I lied faintly.

I motioned to George frantically. 'It's Mr Apsley. Do speak to him. He's such a nice, quiet little man.'

'Doesn't get much chance to be anything else, I expect,' muttered George as he reached for the receiver.

'George Melrose speaking . . . yes, Mr Apsley? . . . mm . . . quite . . . yes, my wife's *very* fussy about the welfare of her horses . . . mm . . . I understand, it's an emotional business buying a first horse . . . well, er, I don't see why not . . . all right . . . yes, a cheque will do. We'll see you about four then. Goodbye.'

But it was early evening by the time an unfamiliar Land Rover, complete with horse-trailer, arrived, driven by a total stranger. I recognised Mr Apsley instantly as he scrambled out of the back with his son. His hair had receded somewhat since our last meeting, but was amply compensated by a luxuriant growth of beard and moustache which gave him a more distinguished look than I remembered.

'Thank you,' he said simply as he handed George a cheque, signed this time I noted, with painstaking neatness and different initials.

'Come on, son,' he urged the silent Trevor, trying desperately to hide red-rimmed eyes behind sun-glasses, although the sun had long since gone, 'ask Mrs Melrose's permission to load him. You'll have to get used to handling him yourself now.'

A bewildered Pitch stopped dead with astonishment when Trevor led him to the ramp. There was something odd and unfamiliar about the atmosphere, and why was everybody watching him like that? His young friend seemed to want him to walk up into that box-like thing. At least, it *looked* like his familiar box, with nice, clean straw and he could smell fresh hay inside somewhere. But why was it so friendly with that four-wheeled monster, keeping so close to its tail as if there were flies about?

He looked round for George. *He* would know. And there he was, standing quietly saying nothing, but with that funny sad atmosphere all around him too.

He placed an uncertain foreleg on the ramp.

'Walk on, there's a good lad,' said George, his voice strangely husky.

Pitch gave him a long steady look, brown eyes searching and trusting, then walked straight into the box. It was a look that was to haunt us for the rest of our lives.

It was to be several months before I saw the Apsleys again. We were returning from a quiet afternoon drive when the sound of a loudspeaker in a nearby field broke through the drowsy hum of the engine.

'Looks like some sort of Horse Show,' said George, his eyes roving over the semi-circle of cars, horse-boxes and trailers.

'Let's pop in,' I said on an impulse, 'it's ages since I went to one.'

'It's fairly late, most of the events will be over by now, but yes, let's have a little wander round. Better take your stick. The ground is bound to be uneven.'

Inside the gates the final heats of the gymkhana were in full swing as ponies of all shapes and sizes pelted up and down to the whoops and cheers of their youthful owners.

We stopped to join in the applause as a diminutive palomino

came in with an elfin-like child on its back, a full length ahead of all the others. I looked up to see a well-dressed young woman with peach-coloured candy floss hair hailing me from one of the boxes, unrecognisable behind enormous sun-glasses. But the voice was unmistakable.

'Mr and Mrs Melrose, what a LOVELY surprise. Did you SEE Sandy?'

'Sandy?'

'Oh, of course, you don't KNOW do you? We changed his name to Desert Sand – his COLOUR you know. And of course, he IS part Arab. Quite clever, don't you think?'

'Most ingenious,' I murmured. Pitch was part thoroughbred, not Arab.

'It sounds so much better when they announce it. And let's face it, he's ALWAYS being announced! We've got a whole WALL absolutely COVERED with rosettes. Come over and see him. He's not loaded yet.'

There against a high hedge was the inevitable white Jaguar sporting new midnight blue seat covers, which exactly matched the paintwork of the horse trailer attached to it. Close by, head hanging rather low beside an untouched haynet, stood a horse, almost hidden beneath the very latest in horse gear: poll guard, knee pads, mane hood, tail guard and initialled travelling rug in midnight blue. A much slimmer, taller Trevor was binding the third of a set of leg bandages. He nodded briefly, and the grey eyes he had inherited from his father, were now tinged with more than a hint of his mother's arrogance and self-importance.

'We got two firsts, a second, two thirds and a fourth today,' he said. 'Bit of a disappointment.'

'He usually does MUCH better than that,' cut in his mother smoothly, 'but I think he's a bit TIRED today. The vet says he ought to be rested for a while, but he's booked for THREE more shows yet. He's got terrapins or something, and needs splints, but he'll have to put up with it a bit longer.'

'Thoroughpins, Mum,' corrected Trevor, his freckles engulfed in a deep flush. 'And he doesn't need splints, he's *got* them.'

'Has he?' she looked vaguely at the leg bandages. 'They're making quite a name for themselves. EVERYBODY'S talking about Trevor and Desert Sand. We try to attend at least two shows a week; Trevor's DETERMINED to get to the top.'

'But isn't that rather a lot for such a young horse?' I said, my heart suddenly heavy.

'Oh, he can take it – he's always game. He was Reserve Champion once. He would have been SUPREME champion but for another horse almost exactly the same colour – but not NEARLY as much – what do you call it, Trev?'

'Substance,' supplied Trevor. 'Sandy should have got it really, but I think the owner of the other one was a professional, or knew the judges more likely.'

'It's name was Oscar, or something silly like that.'

'Couldn't have been,' grunted Trevor on the fourth leg bandage. 'I saw it in one of the Mares' Classes, but it was almost Sandy's double.'

George and I exchanged a glance, our shared secret unspoken. George had remained silent during this dialogue, and now he moved over quietly to the motionless horse.

'Hello, Pit – er – Sandy, old chap,' he murmured. 'Do you remember me?'

But there was no snuffling welcome, no recognition in the brown eyes. They glanced briefly at George and then back into the distance, listless, tired, detached. The eyes of a willing young heart betrayed.

10 · Posy

It was one of our special Sundays – special because we were doing nothing special. I was in my housecoat, feet up on the Chesterfield, engrossed in a colour supplement, and George, in his favourite pullover, one hole per elbow, was sitting on the floor, his back braced against an armchair. Old Mamie was using his ankles as a convenient chin-rest.

Outside, it was a dreary February day, the leafless trees swaying violently under an icy wind. Inside, the log fire threw out a glowing warmth that made us drowsy with togetherness.

'Have you ever thought,' said George suddenly and with a studied casualness, 'that breeding horses might be as interesting as riding them?'

I knew the deep-seated reason for the question. We had seen my latest set of X-rays two days before, and neither had mentioned them since.

I played my part.

'What had you in mind,' I asked brightly. 'Racehorses or Clydesdales?'

But George was seriously intent on his reading. 'It says here the Exmoor is now an endangered species. It was nearly wiped out during World War II, partly because it was slaughtered for meat, and partly because the moors were used as a tank training ground. Apparently quite a lot got picked off by trigger-happy soldiers.'

'Deliberately?' I was horror-stricken at the thought.

'They're having trouble building up the breed again with so few good stallions and brood mares.'

'Does it say anything about their size?' I was familiar with Dartmoors and Welsh, but had not to my knowledge ever seen an Exmoor.

'Yes, er, here it is. 12.3 hands for stallions and only 12.2 for mares, but they can carry a full grown man with ease. Some chap weighing fourteen stone rode one eighty-eight miles in 1820 and beat the stage coach.'

He held up a large, front page photograph. A row of intelligent dark eyes gazed serenely back at me, tiny fluffy ears almost hidden in thick, rich manes which contrasted dramatically with the mealy-white muzzles. They looked small, but compact and sturdy.

'I expect their size is their downfall for planned breeding,' I mused. 'Not many men – or women for that matter – want to be seen on a 12.2 pony.'

'We could specialise in well-handled, well-schooled ponies for children,' George hinted. 'Or they could be used for driving. It says here they are one of the oldest species on record. The Romans used them to build Hadrian's wall, and they probably pulled Boadicea's chariot.'

We both gazed into the glowing fire. Mamie twitched and grunted in her sleep, hard on the track of a phantom quarry.

'There must be an Exmoor Society. I could contact them if you like.' George was determined not to let the matter drop.

But I was already hooked. In the flickering flames I saw visions of terrified ponies fleeing before army tanks or dropping dead and bleeding under a hail of gunfire. Yes, I would do my bit. There was no lack of space now, and 'living out' ponies would only need a watchful eye. Suddenly I had a new purpose in life.

'I'll try and find out more this week,' I said. But George got there first. He arrived home with a scribbled address.

'I've found them,' he called from the garage door. 'They're sending a list of contacts, and I've asked for details of joining the Society.'

There were plenty of members, when the list arrived, but very few prepared to part with a registered mare or filly. With growing disappointment we made our way down the few telephone numbers provided. I was thrown completely off guard when I finally got the answer yes. A Mrs Mitcham had that very morning been let down over the purchase of a filly. She was moving house shortly to a place where there was not enough 'keep', her brood mares had already gone to good homes, and now she was left with a forlorn little yearling. It was a classical example of its breed, registered as such, and of a gentle, kind nature. Unfortunately she lived, not surprisingly, a long way away in Exmoor, and the weather was appalling, quite unfit for travel.

I was desperately anxious to clinch matters.

'I'll send you a deposit and personal references if you like.'

'That will be all right,' she sounded friendly but harrassed. 'Fifty pounds will do, but we'll have to get her to you by next month when we move. Never mind the references. I've heard about you from the Society.' I wondered what elaborate details George had supplied.

There followed a long spell of unabated bad weather and frequent telephone calls – always at the cheap rate. We kept each other informed about road conditions at our end of the line, exchanged cures for winter ills and recipes for inexpensive meals, discussed the recession, the plight of the Exmoor and the problems of moving house and generally became firm, if invisible, friends.

I learnt that they had a seven-year-old son and were moving

North only because her husband had been transferred to a better job with his firm, that the new house was a delightful 'listed building' but its one drawback was the lack of land – a mere two acres with a single loose box – and that her one regret was that she would now be unable to follow out her original plan of starting a small herd of Exmoors. She was particularly anxious that the solitary Midge, the yearling, would have company, as she was already showing signs of pining. I assured her we had two gentle mares, one of them a small Welsh mountain pony, about the same size as an Exmoor, and that the little filly would be in good company.

She was suddenly keenly interested. Was the pony rideable?

'Oh yes,' I replied. 'Very much so. We used her for the very young beginners.'

The question came out of the blue.

'I don't suppose you would consider a part-exchange, would you? Barry is desperate to learn but, of course, our Exmoors were unbroken.'

'Why not?' I was delighted with this unexpected turn of events. 'You can see Posy when you bring Midge and take her straight back in the box if you like.'

Posy had been the baby of our establishment, not in age but size. Standing only 12.1 hands high with a rich chestnut coat, she had come to us when her owner was obliged to forfeit grazing rights to a new housing development.

We had fallen in love with her at first sight; with wide-set eyes, a neat, sturdy body and an abundance of flowing mane and tail she was every child's idea of a perfect pony. The briefest test had shown instantly that she was well-schooled, impeccably mannered, could jump without fuss, and like the long-departed Patchy, had the uncanny ability to 'look after' a nervous young rider.

She had proved to be a remarkably versatile animal, would live in or out, eat anything offered and even doubled up philosophically as a little pack-horse, carrying piles of folded blankets or stacked New Zealand rugs on her broad back with infinite care, whenever Rosemary was in need of some general assistance.

When it came to grooming lessons for the uninitiated, Posy was the ultimate Visual Aid. She would stand like a small equine statue while inexperienced hands brushed her coat clumsily, dragged tangles out of her mane and tail, and even crawled trustingly underneath to chip mud off a fluffy belly. She solemnly raised each hoof – in strict anti-clockwise order – so that it could be picked out thoroughly, and often nodded off peacefully as the hoof-oil was finally daubed on with a wobbly brush. She would continue to doze on, automatically receiving the bit, or dropping it out again, as reins got twisted round her ears, or the throat lash ended up down her nose.

But despite her size and patient co-operation she had soon made it plain that she was not to be underestimated, and firmly took up her place in the hierarchy of the paddock, often curling up like a cat on the path to ensure that she was first in the hay queue.

All of these details I gave glowingly to Mrs Mitcham as we waited for the treacherous weather conditions to abate. We were just on the point of exchanging good knitting patterns for polo-necked sweaters when suddenly it happened – the weather man on the television screen approached his chart with a cheerful, relieved smile.

At 7.30 the next morning the telephone rang. 'I've checked the travelling conditions at *both* ends,' Mrs Mitcham almost shouted. 'We're on our way, if it's all right with you!'

It was the daintiest little creature imaginable that walked nervously down the ramp in the cold grey of that afternoon, brown eyes enormous with apprehension; but the same could not be said of the person who led her out.

Telephone voices have a way of conjuring up their own special image to the listener, and Mrs Mitcham's homely chats and anxious anticipation of her forthcoming move had somehow conveyed to me a picture of pretty chintz curtains, a pine kitchen and a comfortably rotund figure in apron or bulging jeans wafting an air of home-baked bread. The unknown Barry, I had learnt, was a delicate child, prone to asthma, and would be well cosseted by an anxious, fluttering mum.

But Mrs Mitcham was none of these things. Of Amazonian proportion, she must have been approaching six feet in height, wore enormous Wellington boots and a bulky, sheepskin jacket. Her strong but handsomely bony face had the leathery complexion that told all too clearly of the rigours of life on Exmoor. As she led the filly forward the contrast made the tiny animal seem even more vulnerable and forlorn.

'At last!' she boomed, and I was forced to the conclusion that there must have been something very amiss with her telephone line that so much vocal volume had not reached me before.

'One hell of a journey! But we're here. Isn't she a little beauty?'

It was an apt description indeed. Midge had a rich brown-black coat of exceptional density and length, a tail that reached the ground and a luxuriant mane which almost obscured her tiny ears and fell forward over the hooded, 'toad' eyes typical of her breed. Her exquisite little black hooves moved with the delicacy of a fawn's, and despite the semi-wild nature of her background, she walked willingly, if nervously, on the leading rein.

'Where do you want her?' asked Mrs Mitcham. 'In or out? She's used to both.'

'She can stretch her legs in the yard paddock for a while,' I said. 'The Welsh pony is in there and a bit of company might calm her down after her long journey.'

Posy was enjoying herself in the yard paddock. It had been quite like old times, all that fussing about getting the mud off her winter coat, but not brushing too deep to disturb her own built-in layer of warmth underneath. They had even tidied her mane and tail a bit, and put some of that black stuff on her hooves. Oh, the memories it brought back! Pity there were no youngsters about to crawl underneath. The Stable Yard Boss got annoyed when they did that, saying that it was dangerous because ponies' movements were unpredictable. Unpredictable? Her? It used to amuse her to stand absolutely still for *ages* just to prove they were wrong.

She missed all the activity; it was nice being the special pet. But today two of them had fussed over her again, although the one with the stick was pretty useless – no strength in her dandy brush at all. Still, it was good to be back in the yard paddock, in sight of the big house, and there were even some patches of fresh grass showing through the hard ground.

She looked up at the sound of voices. Three people were approaching: a little one (the Stable Yard Boss) the middling one (wobbling on her stick as usual) and a giant. And the giant was leading – no! it couldn't be! – a *pony*, a little slip of a thing, all cute and baby-faced, and they were all fussing over it.

'There's the pony I told you about,' I said to Mrs Mitcham as we approached. Posy was standing absolutely still, four square, ears pricked and alert – a perfect example of a Welsh Mountain pony.

'Very nice indeed,' said Mrs Mitcham, 'I would like to see your girl ride her if I may.'

'My girl' was already making her way to the tack room. Rosemary was light and petite enough to ride Posy, and had often declared that, had Posy been a *little* bit bigger, she would have liked to buy her herself.

I opened the gate and Mrs Mitcham led Midge in. The tiny filly, released from her headcollar took a few uncertain steps towards the stationary Posy. She was trembling slightly, her nostrils dilated. Posy remained motionless.

'Walk on, there's a good girl,' coaxed Mrs Mitcham. 'Go and say hello to your new friend,' and she patted the pony's rump with a bony hand and gently removed a few stray wisps of straw from her tail.

Posy was watching intently. So that was it! Thought it was going to move in and steal all the fuss with its great big eyes and silly putty-coloured nose, did it? Well, we'd soon see about *that*.

She laid flat her ears and charged.

Midge was just as fast. She swung round and fled, the pair of them careering round the small paddock at breakneck speed. Clumps of frozen soil were thrown into the air and Mrs Mitcham and I retreated hastily back through the gate. They were well matched, Posy wily and experienced, Midge nimble-footed and endowed with extra speed of sheer terror. Rosemary returned with the tack just as the two reached the far corner almost simultaneously.

'Oh no!' she gasped. 'She's going to *corner* her. Oh, she mustn't do that! Pose-ee-e!' she yelled at the top of her voice.

Sure enough, the wily Welsh pony had manoeuvred the filly until she was trapped in the triangular apex of the post-and-rail fencing, and we watched horrified.

But Midge was a born survivor – hadn't her ancestors proved it? Her grand-dam had told her how, out on the moors, they had outwitted the great metal giants that snorted fire and thunder and ate men, carrying them around in their insides still living. So who was this fat middle-aged nobody anyway? She turned her little rump to Posy and let fly a barrage of kicks from her tiny hind hooves. Posy stopped abruptly, not because it hurt particularly, but because it was not quite what she had expected. In that instant Midge twisted her slim body literally under her opponent's chin and was away again.

Rosemary dumped her load of tack unceremoniously and shot forward to Box 4 opening the door with a swift movement of expert hands, then closed it smartly again after the small, sweating body, sensing safety, had rushed in.

Posy thundering only a few feet behind skidded to a halt on the concrete paving, ears flat with fury and nostrils wide. Could it be that the Boss was on its side, too, after all they had done together?

She charged around the perimeter of the paddock again in sheer frustration, and then she saw her chance. She would show them.

The gate leading to the spinney had long succumbed to metal

fatigue in its ancient hinges, and, being rarely used now, had been temporarily replaced by an out-of-work wheelbarrow lying on its side. 'Just as a deterrent,' George had said. Posy made for it at full speed, cleared it effortlessly, and disappeared into the tangle of the spinney. The ghost of the departed Bracken flickered across my mind's eye.

There were a few moments silence, broken only by the filly's exhausted blowing on the other side of the stable door.

'Is that the pony you said was so quiet?' asked Mrs Mitcham in an oddly strained voice.

Rosemary was picking up the scattered items of tack.

'If I hadn't *seen* it,' she said faintly, 'I simply wouldn't have believed it. It must have been sheer jealousy. I've never seen anything like it.'

'I've never seen anything like it either,' said Mrs Mitcham drily, and I had the uncomfortable feeling that she no longer believed a single word I had said on the phone.

But Midge at least was safe. My main concern now was for Posy.

'How far can she get?' I asked Rosemary anxiously. 'Are any of the gates open?'

'Only the one into the near paddock. After that she can't go any further. She'll probably tire herself out and come back.'

She prepared to replace the tack; we both knew without a word being spoken that Mrs Mitcham was no longer interested in seeing 'my girl' ride our quiet Welsh Mountain pony.

Half an hour later Mrs Mitcham was gone. She simply *had* to get back, it got dark so quickly and she couldn't possibly wait until we rounded up the pony. So perhaps a straightforward purchase of the filly would be better after all?

I gave her the cash and received Midge's Registration Certificate in exchange. In spite of her arduous journey, she had not waited long enough to accept a cup of tea, let alone the snack, together with some selected pet recipes, I had intended to offer her.

I needed that cup of tea badly myself though.

'Come and join me, let's unwind together,' I said weakly to Rosemary, who was gently calming the frightened youngster.

'I think there's someone coming,' she commented as she removed her boots at the door.

A tiny figure was peddling furiously up the drive on a miniature red bicycle. I recognised her immediately. She was the small child whose parents' home backed on to one side of the large paddock beyond the spinney. A winsome little creature with ash blonde hair, we often saw her over the hedge from our vantage point on horseback, as she swayed backwards and forwards on her swing accompanied by a large toy panda. Nearly all our horses had had to be initiated into the mysteries of the sque-eak-groan, sque-eak-groan of the invisible swing and the child's incessant chatter with 'Thammy'.

'Hello,' I said, 'what's your name?'

'Pip.'

'Well, Pip, it's nice to see you on our side of the hedge for a change.'

But Pip had no time for preliminaries.

'Mummy thayth your pony'th eatin our garden.'

'Our pony's eating your garden? How did she get there?'

'Through the hole.'

'The hole? I didn't know there was a hole.'

'In the hedge. Thammy made it. Well . . .' she traced a pattern on the brickwork of the porch with a stubby finger, 'I *helped* him, of courthe.'

This was an unexpected turn of events.

'Rosemary,' I said urgently, 'Get a headcollar quickly.'

'Mummy thayth,' cut in Pip, 'if you'll thend a head-um-collar we'll bring the pony back for you.'

'That's all right,' said Rosemary, 'it will be easy to –'

'Thammy thayth *he* want-th to come too. What'th the pony'th name?'

'Posy,' I said, 'but she –'

'Pothy . . . Pothy . . . I like that name,' whispered Pip to herself. 'Thammy'll like it too.'

A quick reference to the telephone directory and a call to Pip's mother confirmed that she had indeed sent the child.

'Do give her a headcollar, Mrs Melrose. We would love to bring the pony round. It would be a little treat for her. She's always telling her beloved Sammy about the ponies on the other side of the hedge.'

'But how is the pony – er – behaving?' I asked anxiously.

'Quiet as a mouse. Seemed to let off steam in the paddock for some reason, then popped in here through a gap in our hedge for a quick snack from the jasmine.'

When the trio arrived it was not quite the combination we had expected. Posy, her coat streaked with sweat and looking not a little shamefaced, was walking quietly beside Pip who held the lead rein importantly. Sammy, the panda, sat lop-sidedly on her back, his nose tilted absurdly into the tangled mane. Pip's mother, who looked little more than a teenager herself, with the same ash blonde hair falling over her shoulders, held the battered old toy in place. It was a pretty, family scene, worthy of a camera shot.

'Something seemed to have upset her in the paddock,' said Pip's mum, 'then she *crawled* under our hedge on her belly and walked straight up to Pip. She's in a bit of a mess, I'm afraid.'

'We'll put her in a box until she dries off,' said Rosemary as we exchanged astonished glances, 'then I'll brush off all the mud.'

'Can we come too?' asked Pip. 'Thammy want-th to watch.'

'It'll take quite a long time to dry I'm afraid, but you can come and settle her in.'

Rosemary had already prudently removed Midge from the stable yard and introduced her tentatively to old Ria in the far paddock – well out of sight and sound of her enemy. The two had snuffled each other cautiously then walked away side by side to the far end of the field where Ria introduced her new charge to the best pile of hay and the water butt. It was a relief that they had taken to each other so naturally, Ria with a new little waif to mother and guide, and Midge sensing safety with the old mare and her comforting dam-smell.

In the box Posy stood bedraggled and dejected with only the occasional enquiring look at Pip.

'Look mummy,' said Pip suddenly, 'She'th got twig-th th-tuck to her tummy.'

Without a trace of fear she bent to remove them, gradually crawling under the hairy belly.

'Pip, don't do that!' her mother cried anxiously; 'It's dangerous.'

But the pony stood stock still, only bending a neck gently to snuff at the ash blonde locks as they appeared briefly at each side.

'She'th *very* dirty,' Pip said severely rising suddenly on Posy's offside. 'Can I come and help to clean her? Thammy thayth he'll help too.'

'Why not?' smiled Rosemary. 'I'll keep an eye on her, just for an hour or so.'

'Well . . .' said Pip's mum, 'if it won't be too much trouble. I think she gets a bit lonely playing by herself most of the time – and I've got a lot to get on with myself.'

She certainly had. She and her young husband had earned the grudging respect of the village by buying a plot of land and setting about building their own home, brick by brick, tile by tile, while carrying on their daily lives in the confines of a temporary caravan. It was proving a long and arduous task, fraught with unseen difficulties and rising expenses; and both, though young and energetic, were beginning to show signs of strain.

The next morning the red bicycle reappeared with Sammy, the panda, strapped to the back. Pip carefully unfastened him, tucked him under her arm and went in search of Rosemary. Rosemary – ever the willing teacher – sat him carefully on a bale of straw 'so that he could supervise'. Posy was now firmly established in Box 1 and the yard paddock, well away from the source of her jealousy, and she went through her Visual Aid routine to perfection.

Soon Pip and Sammy were regular visitors. Child and pony had a natural empathy, and the little girl chattered incessantly to her new charge as she had once done with the now neglected Sammy. More and more he was forgotten as he sat on his bale of straw, and on several occasions even remained strapped to his seat on the bicycle. Then came the day he was nowhere in sight at all.

Pip's conversation had taken on a new trend.

'Pothy thayth her water bucket'th empty. Pothy thayth her legth are *very* dirty today. Pothy want-th to go for a walk round the paddock . . .' And then, inevitably, 'Pothy thayth why don't I get on her back like the other-th uthed to do?'

It was a Very Important Day indeed when Pip, escorted by a proud mum, arrived in diminutive jodhpur boots and somewhat top-heavy hard hat, the ash blonde hair tied with pink ribbon in two neat little bunches.

'I'll have to get her jodhpurs later,' said her mum avoiding my eyes. 'I couldn't – er – get the right size. I hope the jeans will do for the time being.'

Up in the saddle, Pip was given the first basic instructions: heels down, hold the reins correctly, sit deep, back straight, and Rosemary took her forward on the leading rein. Posy walked delicately and carefully as if on eggshells. In no time at all, it was obvious that the leading rein was superfluous. Pip was sending gentle messages with her heels and her hands and Posy was responding.

'It's quite extraordinary,' Rosemary said later. 'You don't *teach* that child, you just show her, and within minutes she's got it. She's a born little rider with a natural seat. And another thing,' she added, dropping her voice uneasily. 'I swear those two do actually *talk* to each other. It's quite uncanny.'

When the bitter cold winds finally gave way to warmer, sunnier weather and the mystic rites of official British Summer Time were firmly established, Rosemary arrived one morning with a sheaf of papers.

'I've been looking at the schedules for some of the first local shows,' she said wistfully. 'It would be nice to be involved again, if only in a minor way.'

I had sensed a growing restlessness in her for some time. I knew she missed the competitive spirit and atmosphere that had once kept us all on our toes, and a nagging little anxiety began to tap at the back of my mind.

She was running a practised eye down the lists of classes and events.

'Mountain and Moorland . . . mm . . . small breeds . . . mm . . . leading rein . . . registered and unregistered . . . mm . . . turn out . . . handy pony . . . mm. Why don't we take Pip along just for the fun of it? It would be something to plan and look forward to, and get us back into the swing of things. There are several classes she could be entered for here, and the first show is only about half a mile away. It couldn't be better!'

I was immediately caught up in her enthusiasm as was Pip and her mum, while Sammy, we were informed thought it a 'thuper idea'.

Pip's daily instruction now began in earnest; even play school was occasionally curtailed to fit in with Rosemary's schedule. A mock-up show ring was pegged out in the yard paddock and Rosemary – delighted to be back on familiar ground and with such a willing pupil – explained the importance of correct procedure, good manners, and neat appearance, and gave all the other little tips she could think of that came from years of experience and enthusiasm. The child, her mother and the pony all listened intently.

The day of the show dawned clear, crisp and sunny.

'A good omen, maybe?' smiled Pip's mother nervously as she arrived in businesslike jeans, boots and sweater almost simultaneously with Rosemary at 7 a.m.

Posy had been meticulously shampooed the night before, rugged and left in deep straw. The first class for which we had entered Pip – MOUNTAIN AND MOORLAND, SMALL BREEDS, REGISTERED AND UNREGISTERED, IN HAND – was scheduled for 9 a.m. Preparation and grooming was now a serious business. She was brushed and re-brushed till her coat shone like satin and each individual hair of her mane and tail glistened with its own pristine glory. Hooves were oiled and buffed, the eyes carefully wiped and given a whisper of Vaseline for brilliance. Meanwhile the tack gleamed like mahogany, the leather dark and supple, the stirrups brilliant with metal polish. Through it all, Posy stood patiently still. This was the life!

Pip herself arrived at 8.15 a.m. escorted by Daddy, that mysterious figure I had only seen at a distance over the hedge, lugging bricks up ladders, feeding cement mixers, or sawing seemingly endless lengths of wood. But today the paint-stained dungarees were abandoned, replaced by smart slacks and a well laundered shirt. The young tanned face, prematurely etched with lines from the hours of self-imposed grinding labour, was aglow with pride as he led his young daughter forward.

He had every reason to be proud; she was an enchanting little figure. In her newly acquired jodhpurs and diminutive hacking jacket, her hair neatly bunched behind each ear, she wore a little sprig of white heather in the tiny button hole.

'I hope that's all right,' her father said shyly, offering a work-roughened hand. 'Just for luck, you know.'

When we reached Ring 2 the only composed one among us was the child. Her parents, whose names I now knew were Valerie and David, were visibly nervous. Rosemary was unexpectedly tense and kept whispering last minute instructions in an edgy voice.

'Oh dear, I do hope we're doing the right thing,' she said to me in an anxious aside. 'She's so very young, really.'

I myself felt ridiculously weepy and nostalgic as I gazed around the busy scene – the ponies and horses of so many different types, shapes and sizes, and their young riders so eager and ambitious. I felt superfluous and useless leaning on my stick. But there was no time for sentiment or lost dreams. The competitors for Class 9, Ring 2, were already assembling.

We watched tensely while Rosemary expertly introduced Pip and Posy to the circle of walking ponies, third from the front.

'Now, Pip, just watch what the others do, then you do it – *but better*!'

She stepped back and the pair were on their own, amid an impressive array of Dartmoors, Welsh and Shetlands, all of them turned out to the best of their owner's ability. Pip was, without a doubt, the youngest and smallest handler.

Suddenly, just as the judges were about to commence there was a disturbance as a late arrival rushed through the crowd and joined the circle.

'Oh no!' gasped Rosemary, 'No! I can't bear it!'

The newcomer was an Exmoor, a larger edition of Midge, and its owner, a stout teenager, took up position immediately in front of Posy.

Posy stopped abruptly, ears flattened and tail swishing ominously, but Pip, self-possessed and unruffled, spoke earnestly to her in her childish pipe. No-one among the onlookers heard what she said, but Posy did. Her ears pricked forward again and she resumed her walking crisply and calmly.

As the judging continued it became very apparent indeed that Posy was no stranger to the show ring. We ourselves had bought her merely as a reliable 'schoolmistress' pony for beginners with no particular thought for previous achievements. Now the full extent of her earlier schooling was plain to see.

She stood still but alert when asked, her sturdy legs positioned in the perfect rectangle. She trotted smoothly and evenly, not too fast, not too slow, for her young handler to keep pace beside her on her own immature little legs. Throughout, Pip remained solemnly composed without a trace of that precociousness that all too often mars the aspiring offspring of proud parents.

Finally the judges began to call in the line-up. Pip was called first and, being first, was uncertain as to what was expected of her, leading Posy to the centre of the ring. A smiling judge motioned her to the right. Pip shot an enquiring glance at Rosemary who nodded and pointed a finger. Pip moved Posy along and they stood motionless once again.

'I think . . . I think . . . I do believe . . .' said Rosemary breathlessly, and she was right. All the other ponies called forward were placed to Posy's left, and I thought Pip's young parents would burst with pride when the red rosette of First Prize was handed to their daughter.

Quick hugs all round and a tear or two from Mummy and it was on with the next preparations. It was only a matter of minutes before Class 11 was due. Pip's now dusty little boots were given a quick wipe and an errant hair ribbon re-tied. Posy's coat was smoothed over yet again with a pad of black velvet, and the shining saddle and bridle carefully fitted.

'LEADING REIN PONIES IN THE COLLECTION RING PLEASE' boomed the loudspeaker. 'PONIES NOT EXCEEDING 12.2 HANDS, RIDERS EIGHT YEARS AND UNDER.'

This time the result was almost a foregone conclusion. Pip, the youngest and tiniest competitor who had emerged triumphant unaided from Class 9 now sat confidently and at ease in the saddle with the unfailing Rosemary in charge. The natural seat she had detected so early in the child now manifested itself; despite her tender years she was already that rare and enviable rider who 'seems to be part of the horse'. For the second time she emerged with a red rosette.

Pip's parents were almost speechless with astonishment, awe and delight.

'There *has* to be a third!' said David. 'Things go in threes. I wonder if she'll manage a hat-trick!'

'It's a lot to ask,' Rosemary was busy loosening Posy's girth. 'The opposition in the other classes will be quite stiff, and she must be one of the youngest competitors here.'

Pip and Posy were nuzzling each other.

'Pothy thayth she'll do her beth-t,' said the child.

The hour's wait to Pip's third and final entry seemed interminable. Posy was allowed to graze a little while we consumed refreshments that none of us seemed to taste. David took Pip on his shoulders to see the fine hunters doing near-impossible things while Valerie and I were content to do nothing in particular, keeping an eye on the 'snack and tack' department. Rosemary checked schedules, times, fees and prize money.

'Now,' she said as Class 14 was almost due. 'We've done the serious stuff. This is where the fun begins.'

'HANDY PONY, CLASS 14, DUE TO START IN FIVE MINUTES' TIME. ALL COMPETITORS IN THE COLLECTION RING PLEASE. CHILDREN EIGHT YEARS AND UNDER MAY BE LED, SUBJECT TO HANDLING RULES.'

Pip was wide-eyed with excitement and astonishment as Rosemary explained each of the obstacles that lay ahead. It was a motley collection that lined up for the start, and Rosemary was right; the opposition would be stiff for many of the youthful competitors were mounted and clearly experienced.

Rosemary braced herself for the exertion she knew lay ahead, and they were off: through a maze of zig-zag straw bales, over a low, coloured pole, under an archway of branches, up to a gate, open it, go through, close it again, pick up a letter, post it in a pillar box, jump off your pony, load it with a filled sack, run beside her to deliver it, unload it at the other end, get back on at the offside, duck under a line of washing, pick up a yellow flag and place it in a red cone, pick up a red flag and place it in a yellow cone. The excitement in the onlookers reached fever pitch as the riders dashed, slid and wobbled, missed and tried again, the handlers giving only the minimum assistance as regulations demanded.

Pip clung like a limpet to her mount and again we saw quite clearly that Posy was no stranger to the game. At first it was impossible to guess in the general confusion of figures and movements where each might finally be placed, until at last two emerged well ahead of the others – Posy and a stocky little grey with an equally stocky little rider on its back, his brow puckered with determination.

As they rounded the last pole before the final run to the winning post, incredibly Posy was in the lead. Then disaster struck. She turned so swiftly and nimbly that Pip was swung sideways from the saddle by sheer centrifugal force. Desperately she clung on, minus a stirrup, and true to her instinct Posy stopped briefly to let her adjust. Somehow Pip scrambled back up, but precious moments had been lost. The grey was ahead, and Rosemary, scarlet faced and minus her hat, ran like a hare to do the impossible. The cheers of the crowd grew deafening. The boy on the grey, now confident of his victory, unwisely began to pull up before he reached the finishing line, and the two ponies crossed it simultaneously. Or did they?

All around us opinions were expressed and argued against.

'It was the grey – clear as daylight.'

'No it wasn't, the little chestnut did it by a whisker.'

'It was definitely the boy on the grey. I was standing level with the finishing line.'

'I think the little chesnut should get it anyway for sheer guts. Did you see that girl *run*!'

That girl had all but collapsed into David's arms quite unable to speak, while Valerie helped a somewhat dazed Pip to dismount.

An expectant hush descended on the crowd, then came the announcement.

'IN THE ABSENCE OF THE NECESSARY TECHNICAL EQUIPMENT TO VERIFY A PHOTO-FINISH OR OTHERWISE, THE JUDGES HAVE UNANIMOUSLY DECIDED TO AWARD THE FIRST PRIZE JOINTLY TO THE PONIES PEBBLE AND POSY.'

'You did it! You did it!' said Pip's father hoarse with shouting and emotion. 'You got a hat-trick. You did it!' and he swung his little daughter high in the air.

Pip gasped with delight and caught her breath.

'Not me, Daddy, Posy did it,' and I wondered whether in the

general euphoria, I, the ex-teacher, was the only one to notice the perfectly formed letter 's'.

From that day onwards the exploits of Pip and Posy became legendary in the village and surrounding district. Pip's father 'happened to have a few bricks left' and a loose box was added to the splendour of the new house. Posy took up residence after the exchange of the same modest sum we ourselves had originally given for her, unaware of her hidden talents.

On Rosemary's advice Pip now began serious riding lessons at a nearby Equestrian Centre. She grew taller and a little slimmer, Posy rounder and a little slower, and Valerie wisely restricted their activities to selected local events in view of the extreme youth of the one and the advancing years of the other.

Even so, their appearance at any gymkhana was enough to make other youthful competitors shrug with resignation, and a special shelf had to be put up in Pip's bedroom to accommodate the growing number of cups and trophies.

There, after a hair-raising experience in the spin drier, Sammy the panda, fluffed up with importance, sat permanently on guard.

11 · Chess and Angelo

The big Cremello tossed his head, his nostrils flaring. The wind was rising in the north, and already he could feel the blood coursing through his veins. He banged restlessly at the stable door with an iron-shod hoof. Why didn't someone come and let him out?

Then he remembered. It was a Day-off Day. They always had a different smell about them. He had had his stint on the lunge rein earlier than usual, and the Stable Yard Boss had got through her work very quickly, then left, leaving everything in order and under control.

Everything except the wind, that was. She couldn't control that. Already two of the stacked buckets had bowled noisily across the yard. A tall sycamore was beginning to sway violently at its uppermost tip. A curved branch snapped and fell to the ground, its side-twigs splayed out like spidery legs. Then inch by inch, gradually, stealthily, it began to move across the concrete like some grotesque insect, now creeping, now leaping after an unseen prey.

The stable cats could feel it too. So merciless to their pathetic little victims in the feedroom, they were now wild-eyed and terrified, whirling and dashing like things possessed, as if the very devil himself were after them.

The Cremello rubbed his creamy mane against the stable door impatiently. Those three out there in the paddock – did they even *know* how lucky they were with all that space to move about in?

Suddenly the wind caught up a yard-brush and hurled it violently against a wall, splintering its head into a shower of bristles. The tall nettles along the fence bowed trembling in its path.

The Cremello paced restlessly to and fro, his nostrils widely dilated. That wild, wild wind *was* coming from the north and again he felt the surge of excitement in his veins. He lifted his fine head and neighed loudly. Far beyond the spinney Ria echoed faintly in reply.

We heard that strident, urgent call as we walked towards the stable yard.

'That's Angelo,' said George to Michael. 'The very devil gets into him when there's a high wind. Let him out, and he's like something possessed, yet in his box or the manège he's a different animal.'

'What's his background?' Michael had caught sight of the impressive head at the far end of the yard.

'Thoroughbred, almost seventeen hands,' said George, 'with a pedigree as long as your arm, half of it French.'

Michael crossed quickly to Angelo's box. A slim, fair-haired young man in his mid-twenties, sensibly dressed in neat riding gear, he had come at Rosemary's suggestion to have a look at Chess, the piebald pony.

Rosemary had been hesitant at first, explaining tactfully that money was on the tight side. Michael, a talented young rider, recently qualified, was starting up his own riding school. He needed good reliable animals, but had not, as yet, the necessary finances to buy the quality he would eventually need. Chess seemed to fit his requirements exactly.

Now he stood and gazed thoughtfully upwards, blue eyes into blue eyes. Angelo shook his mane and pawed impatiently. Not that soppy 'Isn't he beautiful' routine again!

'What's he done?' Michael asked softly, and his gloved hand rested firmly on the muscled neck.

'Affiliated jumping and some dressage,' I volunteered. 'His rider was an international competitor but she's left the district now, just as he was ready for Grade B.'

I was aware that I had sighed involuntarily. The departure of Angelo's rider, following a family bereavement, had been a bitter blow. She had been outstanding, establishing an immediate rapport with the powerful gelding, and we had been unable to replace her – not that we could afford to, now.

'Are you interested?' asked George hopefully. 'We could probably come to some arrangement financially if . . .'

'I'm sorry,' Michael said, 'I can't raise that sort of cash just yet – much as I'd like to. We've just sold our house and moved into a caravan at the school to get capital, and it will take the lot to get established. No, we'd better take a look at that riding pony Rosemary told me about. That's more in our line at the moment.'

He cupped a hand under Angelo's velvety muzzle. 'I'll take him out into the paddock for you if you like. He looks as if he could do with stretching his legs.'

'Are you sure? It's a fair walk through the spinney, and in this wind he might be a handful.'

'Don't worry about that,' said Michael, and he reached for the headcollar hanging outside the stable door.

Angelo was taken by surprise. No drooling and fuss? No flinching at his impressive size? This young man had light but firm hands, a quiet but firm voice. The headcollar was buckled on expertly without fumbling and already they were walking through the spinney.

His spirits rose, and the wind in his nostrils made him prance with impatience. He knew, if he chose to, he could lift this young man clean off his feet with a single, well timed rear, but there was something about the authoritative hold, the steady tread beside him, that forbade it.

He liked him. He reminded him of the rider he had known long ago – the one with the feather-light hands and heels like blown leaves. His will had been hers, and they had done so much together. But she had gone a long way away. Try as he would, he could not catch her skin-smell in the air.

'Walk on,' said Michael quietly, a man of few words, and George and I followed meekly. If we had been expecting fireworks, they never came.

But once Angelo was released on the other side of the paddock gate it was a different story. He was away like the wind that had got into his blood, hooves thundering, mane and tail streaming, he seemed to be part of the very elements themselves.

We leaned over the fence and watched. Michael's eyes followed every movement keenly.

'That,' he said softly, 'is my idea of a horse!' He turned away with the merest hint of a sigh, tapping a boot with his riding crop. 'Now where's the other little fellow Rosemary told me about?'

Chess was one of our least successful acquisitions. We had rescued him at the eleventh hour from a run-down riding school, due for liquidation, where he stood, resigned and forlorn, secured by a single tight strap round his scraggy neck, in a stall far too small for him to lie down in comfort.

His one claim to distinction was his unusual colouring. Technically described as a piebald, he was in fact, almost entirely black except for a single splash of white on his back and haunches which ran down his tail in a narrow streak like a drip of white paint. 'The original pinto,' one student had said having carefully looked it up in the etymological dictionary.

Chess had seen it all. Underfed and overworked, he knew the drumming heels, the over-tight girth, the insensitive hands that dragged and pulled, the nervous, the bumptious, the thoughtless, the downright cruel. He had learnt to endure it all with a patient stoicism, and through sheer self-preservation, had developed the fine art of judging a rider's ability to a nicety – only responding when it was absolutely necessary.

He walked slowly over when called. Michael tacked him up expertly, and swung easily into the saddle. Chess found himself urged forward almost before he knew it.

He did exactly what was asked of him, no more no less, trotting and cantering like an automaton, oblivious of the blustering wind, but surprising even himself with an agile leap over a fallen log. Michael looked as resigned as the pony.

Angelo stopped mid-gallop, and stared. Surely they didn't prefer that dullard to him? He reared impressively and charged again.

Look at me! My ancestors were born of the wind and the sea, the Mistral was our brother! He splashed through a low-lying stretch of mud and water, the result of recent heavy rain, spun round, and thundered through it again. The flowing mane and cataracting tail were almost indistinguishable from the flying spray that rose around him.

Look at me! Poets have written of our harmony of hooves, the wild glow in our eyes. I will face earth, air, fire and flood for you! My cousins brave the fierce, black bulls of the Camargue. All I ask is a challenge, and a rider worthy to share it with.

Look at *ME*! If it's what you want, bright ribbons will fly once again from my mane.

LOOK AT ME-E-E!

The fine head was raised, the nostrils flaring, and his strange, wild cry was carried again and again on the rising wind, distant call of the Mistral.

Michael was indeed looking. He reined in the solemn Chess who gazed languidly at the nearest gate post.

'He'll make a good little all-rounder,' he said almost absently. 'Nothing exceptional, but just right for our nervous beginners. I'll have him, but I'll have to pay at the end of the month, if it's all right with you. He'll be sure of a kind home, that I will guarantee.'

He removed his hard hat and brushed a hand through the flattened fair hair, then cleared his throat, flushing slightly.

'I don't suppose . . . I don't suppose you would like your Cremello schooled a bit, would you? I could spare some time to pop over most days. I haven't got a quality animal of my own at the moment. I could do with the practice and there's spirit there – er – going to waste.'

George had remained very quiet and thoughtful through the whole proceedings, and I wondered instinctively whether something similar had already been going through his mind. Angelo was one of our longest residents; we had had him from a leggy yearling, and he was undoubtedly close to George's heart.

He was silent for a few moments then clicked his tongue and clapped his hands sharply. Angelo stopped abruptly mid-buck, shook himself then trotted towards us, the floating action and fine aura of sweat-vapour rising from his ivory body giving him an almost supernatural look. Legend has it that the horses of the Camargue, probable ancestors of many French breeds, rose from the sea, drawing Neptune's chariot. At that moment, I could well believe it.

He nuzzled George and offered an exploratory sniff to Michael. The men fondled an ear each.

'I don't see why not,' George murmured at last. 'Rosemary does her best, exercising him every day, but he needs a strong rider and you need a good horse. It could work out quite well. We'll try it and see.'

The next day saw Angelo and Michael in the manège with all the accoutrements necessary for serious schooling and jumping.

But Rosemary and I watched with not a little apprehension. The one and only time Angelo had had a male rider on his back had been an outright disaster. A well-meaning friend, acknowledged as an experienced thruster in the local hunt, had offered to 'put him through his paces and keep him in trim'. He had taken a firm grip on the reins, dug in well-spurred heels, and found himself executing an inelegant arc over the startled head. Angelo, accustomed to the finesse of dressage and finely-timed show jumping, made it quite clear that ham-fisted morons were not for him.

The young man, outraged at this indignity to one who enjoyed a certain flamboyant notoriety among the ladies of the hunt, made his second mistake.

'No horse makes a fool of me,' he rasped scarlet with embarrassment and anger, and remounted.

But Angelo was muscular, supple, and intelligent. He succumbed solemnly to the unnecessary dig-dig of heels, cantered obligingly round two complete circles, then chose his moment with expertise. A butterfly buck sent his now over-smug rider sailing through the air.

He did not re-mount a third time.

'Bloody dangerous, that animal,' he muttered, wiping the dust from his face. 'Ought to be put down.'

Angelo had stood motionless while Rosemary gathered up the trailing reins. For weeks afterwards, she swore that he winked.

But this time the rapport between horse and man was instant. Angelo, glad to be rid of the boredom and back in serious business again, flexed his neck and responded to Michael's lightest touch. Michael, absorbed and content, seemed to be in a world of his own. Carefully and sensitively he eased the relaxed muscles back into action again; firmly and gently he insisted on a movement exactly when and where it was required. Angelo, the proud and the powerful, yielded up his will. Here was a man it was a joy to obey; and when the moment of challenge came they would rise to it together.

Try as we would, we were unable to feel any special emotion when the day arrived for Chess's departure. He had come to our establishment remote and detached, and remained a loner for a full two years. Despite all our attempts to convince him that humans could and did care, he never once responded to our affection or uttered a call of welcome across the paddock, even when there was food about. Now, still remote and detached, he walked up the ramp into the horse-box, looking neither to left or right. There was a haynet at the far end; that was sufficient unto the day. At least we knew that he was leaving us sleek and well fed, and going to a new home where he would be equally well cared for.

At Michael's invitation, and indeed insistence, we had agreed to travel with the horse-box to see Chess's new quarters, and accept his young wife's invitation to tea.

'We're a bit spartan at the moment,' he said apologetically, 'and the caravan isn't very big, but Sheila's keen to meet you.'

The modest new riding school bore all the signs of meticulous and careful management. The stables were well creosoted against the ravages of the weather; neat piles showed where the clean straw had been carefully separated from the soiled, to be used again, preventing waste; lead reins were expertly fashioned from plaited bale string and were just as efficient as the expensive, bought variety. Some stable rugs were neatly patched or darned to prevent further deterioration, and here and there a hole in a haynet had been carefully mended with twine. A row of immaculate dove-grey plastic bins, firmly lidded, held the various feeds, and a chart above them detailed each pony's diet. An old-fashioned kitchen cabinet, newly painted white, held veterinary requirements, with a list of the contents pinned to the door.

But whatever careful penny-pinching Michael and his young wife had been obliged to do to launch their new venture, it did not extend to the ponies. Sleek and well-groomed, with an abundance of good hay and fresh water, they looked contented and alert. Chess, we knew, was in good hands.

In the caravan his pretty young wife was waiting to receive us. Dressed in faded jeans and a hand-knitted sweater which bore all the streaky signs of re-cycled wool, she was slim to the point of thin-ness, with a sensitive face, dark eyes and hair, and long artistic hands. I knew at a glance whose fingers had executed the careful mending tasks that helped to save the cash.

'I've been looking forward so much to meeting you,' she said nervously, 'if only as the owners of the renowned Angelo. I get Angelo for breakfast, Angelo for lunch, Angelo for supper. There never was a horse like Angelo!' She laughed shyly, poured tea from an earthenware teapot, and offered us some tiny cakes.

'Not very grand, I'm afraid,' she said. I made them myself, and I'm not quite used to the Calor gas yet. But at least it's economical.'

The cakes, as it happened, were light and tasty, the tea a good strong brew enhanced no doubt by its earthenware origins.

I looked around the neat little caravan. Michael's use of the word spartan was well chosen. Everything was functional and plain, the only adornments being a series of finely drawn pen sketches in narrow frames, hung on the off-white walls.

'Who's the artist?' I asked, and knew the answer before it came.

'Sheila,' said Michael as she blushed faintly. 'She was an art student when we married. Now she specialises in Picasso Patches on torn rugs I'm afraid!'

'They're all animals, I see.' I was fascinated by an exquisite miniature of a curled-up tabby cat, every hair and whisker so minutely portrayed that we could almost hear it purr.

'Yes, but when Michael – we – get established I want to specialise in equine portraits. Let's face it, I've got every opportunity to study line.'

While the two men discussed the possibility of Angelo's re-entry into competitive events, she took me on a mini-tour of her work in the cramped space, adding several unframed sketches from a box under the sleeping bunk.

Some of her pictures were indeed equine studies and her undoubted talent was obvious. From the sturdy chubbiness of the child's pony, to the sleek line of the eventer, she could capture the very essence of the animal with a few well-chosen flowing strokes.

One in particular caught my eye, chiefly because the subject matter varied considerably from her usual style. It was a seascape, the wildly rushing waves crested with foam which took on the abstract form of white horses and their flowing manes.

'I'm thinking of framing this one,' she said thoughtfully. 'I call it "Neptune's Horses" – not very original I'm afraid. Michael says it always reminds him of Angelo – but then, *everything* reminds him of Angelo these days!'

For some reason I could not speak. At the back of my mind I heard the wild echo of that urgent call, carried on a northern wind, pale ghost of the Mistral.

I knew the day would come, and it did.

Rosemary arrived early to tack up Angelo in readiness for Michael's schooling session. His visits were becoming briefer and more erratic as his efforts and hard work in his new venture began to bear fruit; but in spite of the complicated jig-saw of his weekly routine he kept a careful record of Angelo's progress, ensuring steady continuity no matter what complications it caused to his personal plans.

Rosemary, delighted to see her big favourite in expert hands did everything possible to have him groomed and ready no matter what time of day. This morning, however, she lingered at the kitchen door, the saddle over one arm, bridle and brushing boots on the other.

'Will it be all right if I change my day off this week?' she asked, her eyes fixed on her burden and not on me.

'Of course. When would you like to go?'

'Well, tomorrow, actually. Michael won't be here and I can leave the two geldings boxed.'

I waited for the usual surge of explanations that invariably followed such a request, but none came.

'Er – something's turned up,' she said vaguely. 'Heavens! is that the time! I'd better hurry, or Michael will be here.'

I watched the slim figure with the bouncy pigtails disappear into Angelo's box and heard his whinny of welcome. The young

Arab, not to be outdone, called to her too. She re-appeared to give him a quick pat and tell him to be a good boy and wait, then disappeared again in search of the grooming kit.

How many times had I stood like this, leaning first on crutches, then on a stick, and now, today on the back of a chair, watching these every-day activities? They were so insignificant and trivial in themselves, and yet the very fabric of normality to which I clung so desperately. Now, there were only two splendid heads to greet Rosemary over the stable doors. I knew in my heart of hearts that the brief conversation at the kitchen door that morning – scene of so many earnest consultations – marked the end of an era.

I wandered aimlessly into the tackroom which adjoined the house for security reasons, the ever faithful Mamie, sensitive as always to my moods, companionably at my heels. The room had two sets of windows. Those to the front gave me occasional glimpses of Angelo and his rider warming up in a complication of circles; to the rear I could see Rosemary patiently lungeing the young chesnut into obedience.

On the far wall, twelve red-painted saddle racks jutted out starkly. Only two had the polished appearance of being still in use. The other ten, with varying films of light dust, were bleakly empty. The morning sun threw their grotesque shadows on to the wall like the forlorn branches of leafless trees.

I glanced at the fading names. An enormous spider with strange speckled legs sat motionless on the word PITCH, her elaborate web, deadly in its intricate beauty, fanned out and across to the next rack labelled TOSS.

'How odd,' I thought numbly. 'Even the insects knew those two were inseparable.'

In the corner an abandoned anorak hung limply on a peg, its creases dusty and grimy, clearly the forgotten property of a departed working pupil. Beneath it a pair of muddy Wellington boots, their cracked toes telling their own story of cold, wet feet, leaned dejectedly sideways. They were tiny. Who had once worked here with feet as small as that?

On the window sill a row of appropriately filled sample jars were carefully labelled, OATS, BRAN, FLAKED MAIZE, COOKED BARLEY, CHAFF, PONY NUTS and SUGAR-BEET – (MUST BE SOAKED). Beside them a folder, once bright blue, now faded to a sombre grey, bore the title 'B.H.S. Examinations and Syllabuses etc'. Above them, outside, I caught a glimpse of Angelo and Michael, engrossed in each other, performing careful shoulder-in exercises. They disappeared briefly at the far end of the arena and re-appeared to execute a faultless volte, before passing out of sight again.

I wandered over to the area once known affectionately by the girls as Collapse Corner. Only one chair was pulled up by the table, the other three were stacked away. A single coffee mug bore the tell-tale brown stains of recent use, the rest hung on their hooks containing the remains of over adventurous insects.

The sugar jar was empty – Rosemary did not take sugar – the coffee jar half full. A rusty drawing pin at the end of the shelf held a faded, curling picture of David Bowie, bearing the unmistakable imprint of a lipsticked kiss. Mamie was sniffing suspiciously at a crumpled piece of paper. I picked it up and straightened it out. It bore the cryptic message, 'Paddock keys – usual place'.

Glancing out of the back window I saw Rosemary, now in the saddle, patiently trying to convince the exuberant youngster that a collected canter did *not* mean an enthusiastic bash along the full length of the fence.

Her Day Book lay on the table. I flicked through the pages filled with her neat records of daily activities and needs. That day's page began with the words 'Ask Mrs M about tomorrow' and was filled with tasks to be done. With a trembling hand I turned over to the next page. It contained a single entry. '10 a.m.' followed by an enormous question mark.

As I looked along the row of discarded tack, painstakingly cleaned, but now encased in clear plastic bags, I heard the clatter of Angelo's hooves returning from his brief session.

'Mrs Melrose! Mrs Melrose! Are you there?' Michael's voice

sounded urgent and excited. I rushed outside and Mamie gave an involuntary woof.

His face was shiny with exertion, but aglow with a new light.

'Were you watching? Did you *see* those flying changes? Every one of them perfect! It's coming back to him – I *knew* it would. Gosh, what a horse! With his jump as well, he'll make a super eventer!'

'Oh, well done!' I managed, happy for him in his boyish delight, and giving both horse and rider a congratulatory pat.

As they hurried on to tell Rosemary the good news, I was left wondering, was it really possible for the human spirit to be uplifted and yet inexpressibly sad at one and the same time?

Two days later Rosemary tapped once again at the kitchen door.

'I'm afraid I've got a mixture of good news and bad news to tell you,' she said tremulously.

'I know. The good news is you've been offered a marvellous job, and the bad news is that I'll be losing you.'

'How did you know? Has someone told you?'

'No, it was just inevitable. Circumstances have changed so much since you came. Horses gone, and pupils gone. You're wasted here now.'

Her good news was good indeed. She had been offered a responsible position in an Equitation Training Centre of very high repute, following the sudden departure for domestic reasons of a senior member of staff. The bad news was worse than I expected: to confirm her appointment she was obliged to commence duties the following week.

She was visibly distressed at this predicament.

'I would like the job, Mrs Melrose, but it means I can't give you the usual period of notice.'

'Take it while the chance is there, Rosemary,' I said. 'Life has a way of doubling back on you,' (who knew that better than I?), 'so don't miss the opportunity. You've stood by me in a crisis, now it's my turn to help you.'

'It was the least I could do.'

'You never did "the least" of anything in your life. You always do all that's asked of you and more.'

'But what will happen to Angelo and Rashir? Michael can't come every day and . . .' her voice broke.

'Don't you worry about them. We'll sort something out. Just leave everything ship-shape and good luck to you in your new job!'

Brave words. I sounded far more confident that I felt. The three days left of her company and help seemed to pass in a flash. She departed in a flurry of mixed excitement and tears, leaving behind a neatly written 'Daily Routine' and a beautiful potted plant, and carrying an enormous box of chocolates and a glowing testimonial from me.

That evening, George and I took stock of the situation – an aged mare and tiny filly in the paddocks, a potential eventer and fiery four-year-old in the yard. George's work kept him more and more in London. I could now manage to walk – within limits – without my stick.

We discussed various permutations of shared routines, all very possible but problematic.

'How often does Michael manage to get over now?' George was poking at the fire absentmindedly.

'Only about three times a week. Now his school is getting busier he can't really spare the time, but he's devoted to Angelo.'

A lump of coal landed in the hearth with a shower of sparks. George carefully replaced it with the tongs and adjusted its position in the grate artistically.

'Have you ever noticed,' he said thoughtfully, 'how the people who *deserve* the best horses are seldom the ones who can afford them?'

I held my breath. Could it be that he was thinking along the same lines that had glimmered at the back of my own mind? I remembered his scepticism and initial annoyance at my own amateur arrangements with Ginge and her friend.

'It has occurred to me,' George said, obviously choosing his words with care, 'that it would be far more practical if Angelo were to be on the spot at Michael's place. They could really get down to it then.'

I kept my voice as level as I could.

'Full livery with schooling is very expensive. I don't think we could afford it.'

George rolled Mamie over and tickled her midriff. She thumped her tail ecstatically.

'I was thinking more of – well – an indefinite loan,' he said, 'with some sort of amicable agreement, of course.'

I almost exploded with excitement and within minutes I was on the telephone outlining the suggestion to a startled Michael, trying hard not to sound incoherent in my eagerness.

When I had finished there was total silence at the other end. My heart sank.

'Are you there, Michael? Don't you like the idea?'

'I just don't now what to say,' his voice was unnaturally husky.

'Just say yes or no. That will do. We can sort out the details later.'

'I'll come over right away, if you like,' he said.

The hallowed hour of the nine o'clock news came and went, while the pair drew up a practical agreement as to who would pay what, when and how. I made innumerable cups of coffee to replace those that went cold while they discussed, agreed and finalised arrangements for upkeep and veterinary expenses, entrance and membership fees, prize money and – hopefully – trophies. I could not resist the occasional quiet smile as I heard George using certain technical terms and phrases, happily unaware that he was repeating those of Barbara Hargreaves' efficient little document, once the source of so much scepticism.

Finally it was written out in longhand to be typed by George's secretary in duplicate, and jointly signed by George Melrose (owner) and Michael Gray (appointed trainer and rider).

For the second time that month we escorted the horse-box to the now steadily expanding riding school.

Angelo stepped up the ramp with panache, resplendent in the usual travelling paraphernalia that accompanies the Very Important Horse. He was sleek and alert. This was the life he remembered. This meant they were going places at last.

At the other end Michael's young student staff were waiting in respectful attendance for him to arrive.

'Oo-oo-o!' said one as he emerged.

'Isn't he beautiful!' said another.

'Gosh, look at the colour of his eyes!' said a third, and memories of The Squire flashed achingly through my mind.

Angelo gave the third speaker a long aquamarine look then stalked regally into his box, to be greeted by an unexpectedly low whinny from the one next door. Chess, the loner, now acclimatised to the comforts of warm stabling in his new home, was actually greeting an old friend.

Silently we gazed at the two haunches side by side as they each turned their attention to the fragrant haynets – one resigned to a life of patient ignominy, the other with the potential, as they say in the horse world, 'to go to the top'.

As we left, Sheila pressed a flat package into my hands.

'We shall never be able to thank you enough,' she said, her eyes shining with restrained tears, 'but I thought you might like this. It's only one of my own pen drawings – not exactly a Michael Angelo, I'm afraid,' she twinkled at her own modest little joke, 'but it's the one you seemed to like so much.'

I knew without looking it was 'Neptune's Horses' painstakingly and neatly framed.

12 · Rashir

Ask anyone what poetry is, and the chances are that you will be told 'words in patterns', or 'words that rhyme'. And they would be wrong.

Admittedly, poetry is found in verse. Wordsworth's was recollected in tranquillity, Keats heard it in the melancholy of a nightingale's song, Shelley saw it as a glowing coal awakened to transitory brightness, and all too often, it was like Burns' snowfall on the river, one moment there, then gone for ever.

But poetry does not need words. It is the perfect arc of a swallow's flight or the timeless serenity of a swan. It can be the breathless beauty of a dancer's poise, the master stroke of an artist's brush, or the haunting phrase of music that lingers in the heart. I found it in the perfect symmetry of an Arab horse.

Rosemary had been quick to sense the bond between Rashir and me, and the therapeutic benefits of his presence. In the dark days after my accident when I could do little but sit by the window, she would bring him round to the front paddock where

I could watch his every mood and movement through the long hours.

'Much better than TV,' she had said brightly, 'and not nearly so many repeats!' but I knew her understanding ran deeper than that.

Strictly speaking, Rashir was not pure Arab at all, for his dam was none other than my beloved old Ria who had survived the rigours of an Argentinian training and the polo grounds. I had first seen him when he was only a few hours old, still sticky and wobbly, keeping close to his dam's protective stand. From the first, it was the unspoken agreement that he would grow up to be my special horse, as Ria slipped gently into well-earned retirement.

Gradually he grew into an animal of outstanding beauty, with the impressive elegance of his splendid Arab sire, but the deep-chested powerful speed of his Criollo dam. The gentle eye, capable of immense serenity in repose, came from old Ria alone.

On that fateful day that changed my life he was only three years old, and as the months passed, slipping into years, I watched him grow and develop under Rosemary's gentle care.

For me he became part of the seasons themselves. In the summer he frisked and played, his coat gleaming with a metallic sheen that changed and shimmered with every slant of the sun's rays. The proud, arched neck, floating tail and elegant hooves moved with all the delicacy and precision of some instinctive ballet. When the autumn leaves fell, he gambolled among them, sending them flying into the breeze, often seeming to vanish from sight as his own chestnut colouring blended into the golden-brown patterns of the trees.

But it was in the winter, when the snow lay, that he held me breathlessly transfixed. With an almost ethereal motion he would float above the crisp white surface with only the hoof-prints to prove that he had passed that way. His glorious winter coat, sharp contrast to the pristine glisten, was now Shelley's glowing coal, and the sudden flame of flaxen mane, the transitory brightness that told all too clearly the fiery spirit smouldering there.

Now that Rosemary had gone, and the serious business of regular schooling ended, a heartbreaking decision had to be made, for Rashir's going would mark not just the departure of a horse, but the final admission of an abandoned dream.

'We have to be practical,' said George gently one day as we stood side by side watching yet another display of equine exuberance, 'if only for the horse's sake. If you are ever able to ride again . . . I mean, when you are able to ride again,' I felt for him in the misery of his slip of the tongue, 'it will have to be something rather staid and quiet, at least for a while.'

He put a comforting arm round my shoulder. 'This young fellow needs to let off steam and throw his weight around a bit. After all, with a high-goal polo-playing mum and an award-winning Arab dad, we can hardly expect him to settle for the occasional quiet hack!'

I knew he was right. Rashir, my Rashir, my heart ached, where can I find someone worthy of you, your power, your beauty, your gentleness?

There was nothing for it, but another advertisement. That way at least we could reach the widest possible range of applicants, and Rashir would only go to a very special person indeed.

But this time my alleged way with words that had brought such unexpected results for The Squire, deserted me. What could I say? 'For Sale, Exquisite Equine Poem, by Special Arrangement, out of Sad Necessity . . .?'

When the advertisement finally appeared in that well known column of the *Horse and Hound*, it gave only the barest information: he was an unspoilt P.B.A. chesnut gelding, rising five, by an Arab sire out of an Argentine dam. Genuine reason for sale.

'I don't think we'll get much out of *that*,' said George testily. By some quirk of typesetting, the wording looked cramped and unimpressive, squashed into an insignificant corner.

He was wrong. The telephone rang at exactly 8.45 a.m. the next day.

The voice was cultured, charming and bore the unmistakable accents of a public school education.

'Has the Argentine mare a polo background?'

'Oh yes,' I said, 'high goal.' I wasn't quite sure what that meant, but the term had been used to us when we bought Ria on her retirement from the game and it sounded impressive.

'I'd like to come over straight away, if you wouldn't mind awfully.'

'I – er – yes,' I said faintly, 'but where are you? How soon is "straight away"?'

'That rather depends on where *you* are.' His laugh was deep and attractive.

I gave him our address in a daze.

'Right ho! We'll be there within the hour.'

George, who had already mucked out Rashir's box, showered and changed into his suit ready to commute, now reversed the process, rang his secretary to cancel immediate appointments, and got back into his work-a-day gear.

'I'll give him a quick grooming,' he said and rushed off to find the dandy brush.

The young man when he arrived was everything that his voice had suggested, and his name, I was not surprised to learn, was double-barrelled.

He was unbelievably good-looking, with a slim but muscular body shown off to perfection in a fine silk shirt, tailored jodhpurs and gleaming leather boots. His well-groomed blonde hair contrasted sharply with a tanned skin that told immediately of the healthy – and privileged – outdoor life. He had candid grey eyes, a square jaw and an engagingly honest grin. He could have stepped straight out of a Barbara Cartland novel.

The same could not be said for his companion. Equally tanned, but with brown streaky hair almost to his shoulders, he wore an open necked check shirt rolled up to the elbows and displayed an expanse of very hairy chest. Faded blue jeans with frayed edges stopped several inches short of open-strap sandals which revealed a fan of not-too-clean prehensile toes. In the conversation that followed, I noticed that he never spoke unless first addressed by the young Adonis.

George led Rashir out. Both men surveyed him in silence.

'Mm-m-m,' said Adonis and ran slim manicured fingers down the smooth tendons. 'We're not frightfully keen on Arab blood for polo as a rule – too independent – but this little chap could well be the exception. Care to try him out, Rod?'

'Sure thing,' said Rod and in that brief phrase I detected a colonial twang.

Indoctrinated as I was to the golden rules of hard hat and firm heels for riding, especially an unknown horse, I was totally unprepared for the next move.

Rashir, too, was taken by surprise. Rod literally leapt into the saddle, hauling on the girth as he did so, clamped his bare heels with a vice-like grip and cantered him at speed through the gate, along the drive and straight into the manège. The young horse was totally confused at this variance from Rosemary's usual insistance on a well-mannered warming up.

But his rider was not. He was, as they say, born to the saddle, not schooled to it. He cantered, turned tightly, stopped, reined back, swung the beautiful young neck up and round sharply, galloped in a tight arc to the right, swerved suddenly to the left, stopped abruptly, reined back again, then turned the now foaming mouth round several times till it almost touched the flaxen tail. Rashir's eyes rolled white with fear and apprehension, but such was his faith in human nature, after four years of trust in us, that he never once attempted a mean trick of defiance to unseat the cause of his distress.

Adonis watched, leaning elegantly with one polished boot raised on the gate. The grey eyes were narrowed with concentration, and twice he crouched to watch the angle of the hooves.

'Thank you, Rod,' he said, and the simple words were not so much an appreciation as a command.

Rod stopped with a single haul of steely wrists, leapt off, and looped the reins casually over the nearest rail. Rashir, as if from instinct or his dam's memory, stood motionless beside it, flanks heaving.

'Jolly good material there,' said Adonis to a rigid-faced George. 'I like him. What sort of figure had you in mind?'

George was playing for time, like me, stunned by Rod's extraordinary performance.

'W-e-ll, we haven't given it much thought yet. He's really my wife's horse and she . . .'

'I'll make you an offer then.' The eyes were frank, the smile engaging, as he named a four-figure sum that took my breath away. I always knew Rashir was a good horse, but I hadn't realised he was *that* good.

George, too, looked non-plussed, and the young man misinterpreted our hesitation.

'All right then, shall we say —' and he added another two hundred.

I came to George's rescue. 'Actually,' I lied smoothly, 'there is someone else interested, and we'd rather not make an immediate decision. May I ring you?'

'Certainly. I'm off to New Zealand at the end of the week to look over some new stock, so if you call me before then it would help. Here's my card.'

A glance at it revealed instantly that his background was as impressive as himself.

'Goodbye then, thank you for being so accommodating at short notice. I look forward to hearing from you.'

He shook hands with us both, the grip firm and friendly, and bowed ever so slightly over my hand with a boyish charm. Heavens, I thought, how many hearts are *you* going to break?

The silent Rod was already at the wheel of the low, powerful sports car and with a zoom they had gone. Neither of them, I noticed, looked back at Rashir, standing forlorn but obedient by the rail, held only by a single untied loop of rein.

George looked at his watch; the whole episode had taken little more than half-an-hour.

'I'll lead him back to his box and untack him,' he said gruffly. 'Then I'd better get going. Do you think you could manage to attend to him after that?'

I nodded dumbly. Suddenly the need to attend to Rashir was as deep a necessity for me as for the horse.

'I must say, that offer shook me,' I said. 'How do you feel about it?'

'I'll have to think it over,' he murmured, but I guessed from the set of his jaw what the answer would be.

In his box Rashir stood with his head low and facing the corner. He did not turn to look as I entered, and there was about him the air of one who had had his first real encounter with the harsh realities of life.

I began to brush him quietly and methodically, wiping away the flecks of foam with a cool sponge and easing out the ridges left by the cruelly tightened girth. As I massaged along the beautiful neck and down his spine with my bare hands, I kept talking, always softly talking, gentle nonsense that was as soothing to myself as to the horse, and gradually I felt the tense muscles relax. Mamie curled up in the straw and dozed off beside us.

He raised his head and tweaked at a wisp of hay, and I produced my trump card – a juicy red apple with crisp white flesh, already quartered for easy crunching. It is amazing what such an offering can do for the morale of a tired horse. He chomped at it thoughtfully then turned his sad eyes and 'whispered' in my ear.

'I couldn't agree more,' I murmured. It was a little trick he had started as a yearling, and we had kept it up ever since.

Mamie and I left him investigating his haynet. Whatever harsh lessons he had learnt that day about humanity, I at least was forgiven.

As I walked slowly back to the house near to exhaustion, physically and emotionally, a figure appeared round the side of the tackroom. I stared at him stupidly.

'Please excuse,' he said, 'I look for Meesis Melrose.'

'I-I-am Mrs Melrose,' I stammered.

He looked momentarily taken aback, and I realised wearily how dishevelled I must look after my unaccustomed and strenuous exercise.

For my part I was astounded. For the second time that morning I was looking at a masculine vision that could have stepped straight out of a romantic novel. If the first young man was the perfect Adonis, this one was the ultimate Don Juan.

He was as dark as the other was fair, with blue-black crisply curling hair and the evenly tanned skin of the Latin American. His velvet-dark eyes, fringed with the longest, silkiest lashes I had ever seen on a man, slanted very slightly upwards, above high cheek bones. ('Bedroom eyes,' an old college friend would have said. 'Watch out!') He wore a single gold ear-ring, and a gold crucifix nestled in the inviting hollow of his brown throat. His elegant jodhpurs and leather boots fitted his lithe, muscular figure to perfection.

'You have the polo pony to see, yes?'

My brain simply would not function.

'How did you know where we . . . I mean . . . I can't . . . I'm all by myself . . .'

(That's a damned stupid thing to say to a total stranger I scolded myself. Visions of lurid headlines in the popular press flashed before my eyes: DISABLED HORSEWOMAN STRANGLED WITH STIRRUP LEATHER.)

He was looking at me intently, and his gaze travelled briefly to my stick.

'I have introducings,' he said in a treacle-dark voice.

His 'introducings' were written on the back of a business card belonging to a local huntsman whose name and handwriting I knew well. Obviously he had recognised the telephone number in the advertisement and acted accordingly.

'Well,' I said weakly. 'He's just been ridden very hard, but if you care to just look at him then come back tomorrow to ride, you are very welcome.'

'Please permit me,' he said, offering an understanding arm, and a sensuous waft of after-shave tantalised my nostrils.

'Please permit me,' as he opened the yard gate, and, 'please permit me,' as he unbolted the stable door.

Rashir was placidly munching at his haynet, the morning's traumatic experience slipping away. He was sleek and shining from my recent efforts.

The newcomer ran an experienced eye over his condition and form.

'Is good horse,' he said softly, 'very nice horse.'

I leaned my aching back against the wall and watched him as he inspected Rashir minutely. What was it about the game polo that produced such stunners? Were *all* polo players like this? Or was it simply that to own a string of polo ponies was synonymous with having money – lots of it – and that in itself guaranteed the best of everything to start with? The mind boggled at the thought of a team of them.

I studied the dark head as he concentrated on some aspect of Rashir's hocks, trying not to notice the way his hair curled in the nape of his neck. Already, in the confines of the stable, the aromatic perfume of his after-shave – or was it hair oil? – was becoming distinctly heady. Steady old girl, I said to myself severely, your *Woman's Own* days are over.

He looked up, and I almost reeled under the impact of flashing white teeth against his own brown skin and Rashir's dark flanks.

'His lex is good,' he said.

Lex? I scrabbled about in my Honours Degree course (First year, Second term, Supplementary Latin). Wasn't 'lex' the Latin for 'law'? Was there some legal requirement about the registration of polo ponies for foreign players? My brain was addled.

'Lex?' I asked faintly.

'Yes. His front lex and his back lex, all very good. No blemish.'

'Oh, of course. He's been well looked after.' My own lex were distinctly weak at the knees – even more so than usual.

He ran a strong hand down Rashir's haunches with a curiously sensuous movement.

'Yes, he is good horse. I will have him. How much money?'

I struggled for composure. Far too many things were happening far too fast.

'Actually, we have someone else interested,' and, gulping, I quoted the figure offered.

He nodded briefly. Clearly the amount was of no particular significance.

'I give more, if you wish,' he said.

Any minute I really would have to pinch myself to make absolutely sure I was not dreaming.

'But don't you want to ride him? He's – well – he's Argentine-Arab cross, and I believe some polo players don't like Arab blood – too much independent spirit in training.' I hoped desperately that I was sounding knowledgeable and business-like.

He shrugged his shoulders with a ripple of muscle under the fine shirt.

'We can make,' he said, and for the briefest moment the dark eyes held a hint of steel.

Those three words cut like a rapier through my fanciful, addled brain.

'I think,' I said, moving purposefully towards the door with the air of one accustomed to bringing interviews to an end, 'you had better make an appointment to see my husband tomorrow. May I have your telephone number?'

'Of course. I give you my card.' He was already opening the door for me, securing the safety catch and offering me his arm. For the third time that morning I glanced at an elegant, printed card. The name was all but unpronounceable; this time the address was c/o an exclusive London hotel.

The long, low car passed Mrs B as she was returning from a shopping errand on her rusty old bicycle, headscarf and coat flapping.

'What was *that*?' she asked, 'Royalty or Hollywood?' Then she searched my face keenly. 'You look all in. Been over-doing it again, I suppose. Sit down and I'll make you a nice cup of tea.'

Dear Mrs B and her inevitable cups of tea, cure for all problems. Little did she realise that it was her sympathetic understanding that was the real panacea.

That evening George and I got out our pile of equestrian literature and studied POLO: RULES AND REGULATIONS OF, and POLO PONIES: TRAINING OF.

'It can't be too bad,' he murmured. 'It says here that games are divided into chukkas of seven-and-a-half minutes' duration, but a pony may only play two chukkas in a game, with a rest in between. That's only a total of fifteen minutes' work. Short and sharp by the sound of it.'

'With the accent on the sharp,' I said. 'My section says that the pony must be imbued with spirit, but not so much that it is capable of independent thought at variance with its rider's.' Was Rashir's part-Arab spirit capable of independent thought? And if so, how would it be broken? I remembered Rod's vicelike grip, and the foreign stranger's melting brown eyes, that hid a stiletto point of steel.

'The rates bill came in this morning. Seems to get higher every time,' grunted George.

'I know.' I was miserably aware of the drop in our joint incomes that my accident had caused. The cash offer we had received was tempting indeed.

George closed his book with a snap.

'Let's sleep on it,' he said.

But I could not sleep. I sat up, switched on the bedside lamp and opened my latest Le Carré thriller. I could not read either.

I drew up my knees to my chin – that was something I *could* do now – and gazed vacantly at the pool of light, my eyes finally focussing on a small glass sculpture George had given me early in our marriage.

It was made by an unknown Swedish artist and George had bought it because of its unusual and brilliant use of faceted edges and sweeping curves. Depending on the angle of the light – natural by day, artificial by night – it could take on a variety of images that seemed to reflect the thoughts of the observer, much in the same way as people often see pictures in a fire. It was quite a while before either of us realised that, suspended in the multiplicity of changing shapes, like the star in a star-sapphire, was the clearly visible image of the Madonna and Child. It had not been bought for any religious reasons, but this discovery, in its ethereal elusiveness, had made it doubly prized.

I gazed at it intently. There, unmistakable in the halo of reflected light, the serene face gazed back at me.

Years of dragging reluctant students in former teaching days through the themes of nineteenth century literature with the underlying conflict between Church and Darwin had converted me – if that is the word – to agnosticism, a state of neither belief nor disbelief. I leaned over and picked the small sculpture up. The tranquil face disappeared briefly, then shone forward softly again as I turned it in my hand.

'Well, Mary,' I whispered, 'if you were what they say you were, and you are what they say you are, then how about inter-inter- what's the word? interceding for me. I know it's only a very tiny problem among all those mighty ones you have to tackle, but please help me find the right person for my lovely, trusting Rashir. Sorry about the phraseology – I don't mean to be blasphemous – honestly! – but I'm a bit out of practice with praying these days.'

When I put out the light, unbelievably the image was still there, suspended in a shaft of light from the moon.

George was just leaving for work when the telephone rang.

'Don't answer any telephone calls today,' he said tersely.

But it rang again and again after he had gone, and I toyed with the idea of taking it off the hook altogether. In the end I picked it up. Why should I be on the defensive? I owned the horse, didn't I? All I had to do was say firmly that I hadn't yet come to a decision about the animal's future.

'Hello, can I speak to Mrs Melrose, please?' Having geared myself for my speech, I was astounded to hear a woman's voice.

'Mrs Melrose speaking.'

'Ah, Mrs Melrose, you don't know me, my name is Sue Yardley. I hope you don't mind me ringing, but I've just come back from an early hack and I met a girl who says she used to know someone who worked for you. I hear you've got a part-bred Arab you would like to sell. I'm keen on Long Distance riding, and I wondered if I might have a look at him. I live quite near.'

For several seconds I seemed to have lost my voice.

'Hello? Mrs Melrose?'

'Yes, I'm here. Is this in connection with the advertisement?'

'Advertisement? No, she didn't say anything about an advertisement. Oh, you haven't *sold* him have you?'

'No,' I said faintly. 'What was the girl's name?'

'I honestly don't know. We only met briefly along one of the bridle paths, but I think her friend called her Marie, or Marion or something like that. Anyway, she gave me your phone number. I hope you don't mind.'

I did not know of a Marie or a Marion, and our telephone number, if it had not been traced through the advertisement, was ex-directory. I leaned over to drag a chair nearer and sat down on it heavily.

'Where do you live?'

'Only five miles away. I could come straight over if you like.'

'You – you'll be very wel- welcome,' I said, and put down the receiver with a trembling hand.

I limped slowly upstairs and picked up the little sculpture. In the cold grey of the morning, it was just an oddly shaped lump of glass.

I liked her immediately. Tall and well-built, her dark hair was windblown from her early morning ride and there were streaks of mud high on her boots. She brought with her a whiff of clean, fresh air, tinged very slightly with the woodsmoke of early Autumn fires, and she had that frank clear gaze and directness of speech that puts the listener instantly at ease.

'I've just put the kettle on,' I found myself saying as if I had known her for years. 'You're just in time for a cup of coffee.' It seemed the most natural thing in the world that she should follow me into the kitchen and help set out the cups.

'I'm looking,' she said, sipping her coffee appreciatively, 'for a horse that is fit, sound and game, but above all, with enough spirit to set up a real partnership in face of hazards. To me, partnership is the thing that really matters with a horse and rider – there's got to be give and take on *both* sides when you've got fifty miles or so to cover.'

I was beginning to like her even more.

Her aim, I gathered, was eventually the seventy-five mile Golden Horseshoe Ride held annually in England. To minimise the dangers of the event becoming a race, prizes were based on average speed and condition of the horse, with strict veterinary inspection at the beginning and then at regular intervals along the route. There were three awards possible, Gold, Silver and Bronze. She had already achieved a Silver with her present horse, now ageing, but a Gold was her real aim.

'And the fact is,' she informed me, 'most of the Golds to date have been won by Arabs or part-bred Arabs – so I *would* like to try yours if I may.'

'He's quite a good-looker, isn't he?' I said when I introduced her to Rashir later.

'That,' she answered, her face strangely serious, 'must be the understatement of the year!'

When she led Rashir out towards the manège he was tense and nervous. What *was* all this about? Where had the Boss disappeared to these days? He had quite enjoyed his daily sessions with her, learning this and that. Admittedly, he'd often played her up a bit – just to relieve the monotony – but he always gave in, in the end, and she *knew* he would. It was part of the fun.

But now, here was another stranger, and if this one was anything like the last – well, he'd been caught off guard the last time; this time he'd be ready for it! That place by the overgrown elderberry would do. They usually got a bit off-balance at that point, having to duck under the branches. So! he would choose his moment! They wouldn't get the better of him a second time. This time he would really *fight*.

He never had to. The stranger sat lightly but firmly in the saddle, gathered up the reins with just the right amount of touch to be comfortable, and they were off, doing the familiar patterns the Boss used to do. Soon rider and horse were thoroughly enjoying themselves.

'Come on, let's go!' Rashir wanted to neigh. 'Out of this silly boxed-in place – out into the fields and woods together. Let's go!'

When Sue Yardley reined in, slackened the girth and ran up the stirrups with expert hands, the radiant smile of appreciation I had expected was not there. She gave Rashir a thank-you pat with an absent, almost sad expression.

'Don't you like him?' I asked, surprised and disappointed.

'Like him? He's my idea of the perfect horse,' she said quietly, 'but I know enough already to realise he's a quality I can't afford. How much are you asking for him?'

I hesitated. 'I haven't really given it much thought,' I lied. 'The polo people have offered a substantial four-figure sum, but I'm not sure I want him to go into polo.'

'Well, that settles it.' She was leading Rashir resolutely back to his box. 'I simply can't afford anything like that.'

I was desperate to keep the option open.

'Don't dismiss the possibility altogether. For my part the home is more important than the price. Perhaps we could come to some arrangement. You seemed to get on so well together.'

In the stable she smoothed away the saddle and girth marks,

and checked each leg and hoof efficiently.

'To be honest with you, I've had to take a part-time job to make ends meet as it is. I can't expect my husband to pay all the expenses of my personal hobby. I couldn't even afford to pay the difference in instalments. What I earn at school just wouldn't be enough.

'Oh, you're a teacher. What do you teach?'

'I don't,' she said.

'You're not one of those terrifying super-efficient school secretaries, are you?'

A dull flush rose from her neck and suffused her face.

'No, I serve school dinners. The hours are short and convenient. So you see, I'm not quite the type of person you were really expecting.'

I recovered from my surprise quickly.

'Good for you!' I said. 'If an army marches on its stomach, then you must be stoking up the "O" levels. One thing is certain, if you have Rashir, his feeds will be properly mixed and on time.'

We walked back to her car in companionable silence. She was clearly relieved that I had accepted this information so unconcernedly, and I had already made up my mind. This was the right owner for my beloved Rashir, but somehow we had to get round the problem of price.

'Look here,' I said, as she fastened her safety belt. 'You have a chat with your husband about the most you can afford, and I'll have a chat with mine about the least we can accept, and perhaps we can meet in the middle. Somehow, I want to keep him out of polo.'

'With a temperament like his, it would be a tragedy,' she said with a resigned little shrug. 'Would you both like to come round tomorrow afternoon? My husband will be at home, and we might be able to come to some arrangement, but I very much doubt it.'

'Good idea, shall we say about three o'clock?' That, at least, was something positive. And tomorrow was Sunday.

When we reached their home, a former small farm with only a modest ten acres or so left of its original land, we were met by an avalanche of happy, barking, woofing, tail-wagging dogs, several curious cats and a benign white rabbit chewing its placid way through its portion of lawn.

Sue introduced us to her husband. Despite their rural surroundings Richard was 'into computers' and had the ready handshake but keen eye of the sales executive.

'As you can see,' he yelled cheerfully over the general din, 'we're rather a vociferous household. All the waifs and strays in the district operate their own intercom and every one is tuned into Sue's wavelength!' Already I was beginning to see the real reason behind Sue's part-time job.

Behind the house were two loose boxes obviously home-made but immaculately kept. I was surprised to see that both were occupied.

'This is Dan,' said Sue, patting the neck of a solemn-eyed liver chestnut, with the pronounced bone structure of the ageing horse. 'He was my very first horse. He taught me all I know, and now he's nearly twenty-four. He'll live out his days with us for as long as he is enjoying life.'

'And this one's Angus,' offered Richard moving to the second box occupied by a handsome black gelding. 'He's Sue's Silver Medallist, but he's getting on a bit now, too, and we don't want to push him. He's done his bit. So it will be occasional hacking and maybe a bit of hunting from now on.'

'But where would you put Rashir if you had him?' George was obviously as mystified as I was.

'We've thought that one out, if the opportunity should arise,' smiled Sue. 'Come inside and we can talk.'

The sitting-room was cosy and inviting with genuine oak beams and horse brasses. I admired the crisp, loose covers made from material based on an original Tudor design.

'Everything has to be removable and washable in this household,' grinned Richard sweeping a strange-looking cat on to the floor where it glared balefully at him with the disconcerting crossed blue eyes of a Siamese, but swishing the tail of a good old-fashioned tabby.

'Now,' he said, 'let's get down to brass tacks.'

With the clear-headed precision of the businessman he outlined their immediate commitments, not least the upkeep of two teenage sons at college ('supposed to be resident but eating us out of house and home every weekend') and the need for another D.I.Y. stable ('because Sue wouldn't dream of putting old Dan down as long as he is fit'). The figure he finally arrived at, with a remarkable frankness, was little more than half of that we had already been offered.

'So you see,' he ended seriously, 'that is genuinely our final figure, and I thought I'd better make it clear from the start. I don't want to waste your time or raise false hopes for Sue. Apart from that –' he added with a return of the grin, 'I just can't face another sleepless night like last night!'

'Can I say something?' Sue's voice trembled slightly over the clatter of cups. 'If you *did* agree to let him come to me, I would be willing to put in writing that under no circumstances would I sell him to anyone else, and if anything should go wrong, so that we were unable to keep him, I would bring him back to you.'

George was silent, absentmindedly stroking the back of the Siamese tabby, which emitted a low droning sound, presumably meant to be a purr.

'Give us twenty-four hours to think about it,' he said.

Forty-eight hours later, Rashir was in his new home.

'Anyone else would say we were sentimental idiots or just plain crazy,' said George as we carefully skirted the bags of cement ready for the new footings, and followed Sue and Rashir out to the paddock.

'I know,' was all I could manage, and squeezed his arm tight.

Out in the field Rashir exchanged greetings with Angus, then he was off, tail aloft like a banner, his flaxen mane gleaming pale against the coppery glint of his coat. He skimmed the edges, throwing up a shower of golden leaves, some of which fell like dapples of sunlight on his back. He tossed his beautiful head, pirouetted like a ballet dancer, then cantered with a liquid, flowing grace back to Sue.

'Good boy,' she said, 'you're going into Angus's box. He won't mind staying out for a few warm nights till the new one is ready.'

Rashir arched his neck and 'whispered' in her ear.

'I couldn't agree more,' I distinctly heard her murmur, 'but it won't be for long.' Neither of them seemed to be aware of our presence.

Long after the fair Adonis had left for New Zealand and his swarthy counterpart had presumably returned to sunnier climes, Sue rang me one evening in a state of joyous excitement.

'I simply *had* to tell you,' she said breathlessly. 'I tried Rashir out on his first long trek today. We did twenty-one miles and he came back as fresh as a daisy. I checked his heart-beat after fifteen minutes and it was absolutely normal. He seemed to enjoy every minute of it, and so did I. He has no behaviour problems whatsoever.'

She was thoughtful for a few moments. 'Isn't life strange,' she added. 'I've no idea what made me take that bridlepath that day. I normally go the longer way, and I would never have met that girl at all. I don't know what made me do it.'

'I do,' I said. 'Well – I *think* I do,' hedging my bets.

It was a mellow Autumn morning, and George and I strolled through the stable yard. My stick was not such a necessity now, but I was glad of his supporting arm.

The boxes were silent and empty, their double doors closed. The contrast in the colouring of the two halves showed clearly where once the tops had been left open for inquisitive heads to look out. Three empty wheelbarrows stood on their handles like sentinels against the walls.

The path through the spinney was dry and crisp underfoot. What a contrast, I thought, to that day, apparently centuries ago, when a poem-quoting bank manager had helped us to track the elusive Bracken.

We leaned over the fence and gazed at the empty paddocks, where already the summer grass had long since lost its vibrant green. In my mind's eye I saw once again Penny Williams's crazy Western capers, and Webster's unexpected response to Sarah's gingery locks. On the slight breeze I heard the ghost of Angelo's call.

But the fields were not entirely empty. Two distant figures emerged from the camouflage of the thinning trees and walked slowly towards us – one rotund and heavy, the other fluffy and small. Old Ria was bringing her obedient pupil to say hello.

'There you are,' said George as we fondled the soft muzzles, 'The past and the future, side by side.'

'George,' I said suddenly, and had no idea where the urgent thought had come from, 'Do you think Ria would let me try to sit on her back?'

He looked anxious and doubtful. 'She hasn't been ridden for some time. She might object.'

'But Rosemary used to exercise her occasionally and she's never done anything mean in her life. She wouldn't harm me.'

'W-e-ll, it's your decision. I suppose it would be all right if you just sat there – always supposing you could mount.'

'I could use the mounting block, and she *always* stands perfectly still for mounting, you know that.'

George's face was tense, but I knew he understood. Little Midge was tempted to a far corner with a bundle of hay nearly as big as herself, and Ria walked quietly back through the spinney with us, led only by a single tuft of her own mane.

While George tacked her up, finding no resistance whatsoever – Ria had long since learnt to take life as it came – I went in search of boots and hard hat. Both were unnaturally clean, and well wrapped up by the vigilant Mrs B. It was some time before I was able to manipulate my right leg into its boot, but I managed it.

In the manège George stood, tight-lipped, holding Ria by the mounting block.

Now what was it the physiotherapy lady had said? 'When stepping upwards use the *good* leg to take the weight.' I stepped up on to the first level of the block with my left leg, then brought the other to join it. I stepped to the second level and repeated the process. I gathered Ria's reins on her withers, and put my left foot in the stirrups, easing my weight up – it was, after all, only another 'step' in a sense. Ria stood motionless. Slowly, stiffly and apprehensively I brought my injured leg round in an arc over the cantle, and down to the other side. I had no idea what happened when it got there; all I knew was the paradox of painful numbness.

'I'll put your foot in the stirrup for you,' said George, and there was a sheen of perspiration on his brow.

Then suddenly, inexplicably we were moving forward in a slow, measured tread, George leading the old horse with studied care. As my back grew accustomed to the rhythmic movements, I felt my nerves relax. If old Ria knew that the leg on her right flank was useless, she made no sign.

Quietly through the gate, along the drive and down through the village we walked. A local gossip let go of her lawnmower in astonishment and it careered away on its own, cutting a swathe down the centre of her lawn. Here and there a net curtain twitched, two cars slowed down, purring respectfully past, and Ria plodded on looking neither to left or right. She had a job to do.

'Would you like to go into the field for a few minutes?' George asked, looking up from beside Ria's ear.

'Yes, why not? It's been such a long time,' I said tremulously.

In the field the hawthorn hedges were already turning golden brown and red berries vied with a robin redbreast in their brilliance. A flurry of bullfinches whirred away almost from under Ria's placid feet.

'Look, George! Just look at those colours!' But George's head had gone. He was walking quietly several steps behind us. Only he knew what it meant that for those few precious moments I was alone with my horse.

Back in the sitting-room I was firmly tucked up on the Chesterfield, glowing with fresh air and pride. If my back and leg ached, it was no worse than usual.

'I suppose you chose the date deliberately,' said George with a whimsical smile.

'Date? What date?'

'Don't tell me you didn't know?'

I glanced at the calendar. They say truth is stranger than fiction and there was the proof. I had taken a brief 'turn round the fields' exactly two years to the day from my accident. My gentlest, most faithful old horse, whose hooves had once thundered to the applause on the polo grounds of Windsor, and dam of the incomparable Rashir, had taken me quietly and with infinite care through the gate. And what was more, I could swear it had stood back respectfully to attention, in its new uniform of creosote-brown, as we passed.

By the warmth of the fire, George sat in his favourite place on the rug, with Mamie at his feet. The table lamp picked out the gleam of the fine grey hairs that had made their subtle but relentless appearance over the long, difficult months. Out in the paddock, Ria whinnied softly to her wayward little waif.

'The expression in a horse's eye is like a blessing on a good man's house.'

I looked out of the window. The long hot summer had already tinged the Virginia Creeper where it hung so long neglected from the eaves. The setting sun caught its crimson edges and made a rosy leaf motif against the deepening blue.